"THE AWAKENING OF LORA ABERNATHY is a cozy, party quest fantasy that brings readers on a magical journey of soul searching and path finding, filled with restless dreams, witty banter, exploring the wonders of companionship and transformation."

Ai Jiang, author of *A Palace Near the Wind*

"This is a story told as much by heart as it is by gut. With raw emotion, Anthony tears apart concepts of identity, belonging, and family to create an experience that will linger with its readers."

Nathaniel Luscombe, author of *Moon Soul* and co-author of *Human Scars on Planet Skin*

"*The Awakening of Lora Abernathy* is a nuanced journey through the deep dark woods of the heart. Featuring a party of lovable, messy characters, it explores both the toothy and celebratory parts of queerness, transness, and disability. If you've ever come out of a DnD campaign with a whole new gender, this is your book."

Avi Silver, author of *Pluralities*

"i love how rich and full of life [the characters] all are. a party getting to know eachother. the woods messing with the cores of their characters, dream sequences rich with backstory, loss, trauma, guilt. FOUND FAMILY!! and so much trans rep…it's been a hot minute since i've been so enamored with a cast of characters and this book has it! my heart <33"

Kienn Nguyen, author of *Dove's Eyes*

"The Awakening of Lora Abernathy is an exhilarating read from start to finish. MJ Anthony's debut novel introduces a wonderful cast of characters that weave into each other's lives in fascinating ways. If you like fantasy with heart, this is a book you won't want to miss."

Sage Evergreen, author of *Best Cat in Show*

"I got so immersed in this story I forgot I was reading. Micah's storytelling voice has a personality of its own, and each character in this book felt like a long lost friend I didn't know I had, until now."

Beatrice Lebrun, author of *Glowrot*

"Intricate and powerful, this book is for anyone who loves their quests and autumnal horror tempered by the coziness of found family and witty banter."

Molly Haniszewski, author of *Beyond the Border Forest: Into the Prawdziwy Las*

"A heartwarming story brimming with vivid details and richly imagined characters, layered with just the right touch of horror."

Lauren O'Brien, author of *Tide Bound*

THE AWAKENING OF LORA ABERNATHY

for Bobby, Sage, and Ziel

the best DMs I've ever had

and for every trans adult who grew up alone

under an unspeakable weight

AUTHOR'S NOTE &
CONTENT WARNINGS:

Reader,

The idea that you may be holding this book in your hands—that it may live on your shelf, in your phone, tucked underneath your arm—does not yet feel real to me.

Many early readers have remarked that *The Awakening of Lora Abernathy* reads like part of a larger D&D campaign, which makes sense considering that that's where each of the main characters (Lora, Tobias, Nic, and Art) began. Most of their campaigns have fallen by the wayside for one reason or another, and so I took it upon myself to write their stories down. I hope that by closing each of their chapters, I can write new ones. First and foremost, I wrote this story for me.

As player characters, each of the protagonists lived in my body long before they lived on these pages. I carved these characters out of my bones and rooted their traumas in mine. Because of that, this book might have some rough shit in store for certain readers.

Throughout *The Awakening of Lora Abernathy*, you will find depictions of:

Chronic illness (specifically **tick-borne illnesses**)
Panic Attacks
Chronic Nightmares

As well as backstory elements of:

Transphobia
Homophobia
High-control religion

There are several nightmare sequences throughout the book which incorporate elements of horror. These elements include **blood**, **injuries**, **drowning**, and **animal death**.

Does (the) Dog die??
It's complicated—but I am pressing my forehead to yours and promising that we are going to be okay.

Take care while reading, and proceed at a pace that is safe for you.

Eternally howling,

Micah J Anthony

More from MJ Anthony:

<u>Poetry</u>
Tending Clay; Unearthing Stars
Unleash the Cosmos: A Space Poetry Anthology

<u>Short Fiction</u>
A Million Spinning Moons
Losing the Stars
Think of Her Fondly
Growing Things

THE AWAKENING OF LORA ABERNATHY

BY MJ ANTHONY

PLAYLIST

good girls — Josie Edwards
Not Forever After — Olive Klug
Magician — Jules of the Tide
annual birthday cry (interlude) — Lizzy Hilliard
empty vessels — Lilli Furfaro
Run Boy Run — Woodkid
Preybirds (Watcher Song) — Rabbitology
Time Machine — Daisy the Great
Gullible's Travels — Soul Asylum
Something Greater —Anna Bates
Heroes and Monsters — Penny and Sparrow
adulting — emlyn
Eavesdrop — The Civil Wars
The Deal — Mitski
New Constellations — Ryn Weaver
Get Home — Bastille
Burn it Down — Daughter
Malaprops — Clem Turner
Gone By Morning — Madilyn Mei
Gods and Teenage Girls (voice memo) — Ky Hollis
Eaten Alive by Wolves — The Narcissist Cookbook
DUST/DIVINITY — Joy Oladokun
Stay My Fangs — Karma and the Killjoys
I Met The Devil — Lila Blue
Dam, Damn — Pater
Nunemaker's Parable — Everybody's Worried About Owen

CHAPTER 1

Lora Abernathy has always been an optimist.

To be fair, for the last several days she's also been a dog. That tends to help—both with optimism and with other, more practical things, like eating and sleeping.

It's also useful for safety. Girls, especially ones living on their own on the streets of a city as crowded and disorganized as Glenhurst, have to worry about men (ranging from creepy to dangerous) and unspoken social rules (ranging from annoying to dangerous—especially when men are also involved).

Dogs can eat scraps from the trash, and the only man they need to worry about is the dog-catcher.

Tonight, Lora's fur is warm and her dog-belly sits pleasantly full of fish scraps tossed to her by friendly dock workers. The evening air has only just begun to turn from winter's chill to spring's balm and has not yet reached the sweltering damp of summer.

She has plenty of time, she reminds herself, curled up in the back of her mind, as the dog pads down side streets and alleys, sniffing this and rubbing on that and requiring minimal input from her.

Lora does not like the dog, but she can't begrudge its usefulness.

A door nearby slams open, and the dog's ears perk up, followed shortly by its nose. Raised voices carry over on a gust of air, heavy with the scents of soup and bread and pie, the kind of human food it knows that Lora craves, somewhere deeper than the need for sated hunger.

They don't have more than a couple scavenged coins between them, but even a drink and a chair and the promise of human company is enough to drive them forward as one.

The dog reaches the door, winding through the legs of departing patrons, and disappears around the corner. A moment later, Lora emerges from the darkened gap between buildings, gaining confidence with every step, one hand braced against the wall as she remembers how to hold herself up in a body this size and shape again.

Like sea-legs, Lora thinks, then amends it to *dog-legs.*

Lora smiles, then frowns, then scrunches up her nose in an attempt to clear the expression all together. It doesn't work, and Lora scrubs at her face with one hand.

THE AWAKENING OF LORA ABERNATHY

All her life she's felt like an open book, emotions dancing across her expression as fast as she feels them. Spending the last four days in a form that communicates primarily with its ears, teeth, and tongue has made it even harder not to let every passing thought show in the quirk of her mouth or wrinkle of her brow.

The door to the tavern opens again, warm light spilling out across the gravel walking path, and Lora pushes herself forward, her balance restored for the moment.

Lora can feel the dog already pacing restlessly in the corner of her mind located just above their (human) right ear, and she throws an imaginary blanket to cover it.

My turn.

Inside, the tavern hums with dusk-time cheer, and Lora slides onto the wooden bench of a corner booth, settling her back against the wall. Silent as a shadow, she lets her eyes skate over her fellow patrons from behind the brush of her bangs.

At the bar, a gaggle of girls dressed for a celebration pester the person behind it to let them order something "off the menu." When the bartender gives in, raising their hands in good-natured surrender, the group kicks up a raucous cheer. One of the girls, decked out in a flower crown and glittering shawl, leans across the counter to kiss them on the mouth and whoops and hollers erupt again.

The corner booth diagonally across from Lora's is occupied by a tiefling dressed for travel, with dark curls and skin a few shades darker than the embers of a fire. He chews on the inside of his lip, sketching in a small book. Lora wonders what he's drawing, but quickly relegates it to mystery and moves on.

In the center of the space, an older man leans across a table for two. Even from here, Lora can smell the bite of *tree* under his skin and recognize the coppery rings of a dryad on the back of his clasped hands. He opens them to his companion, an equally time-weathered character dressed in a mixed style of masculine and feminine elements, their hair long and laced with beads, and reveals a ring in his palm.

Lora thinks of her parents and tears her eyes away.

On her second, vigilant skate across the room, Lora and the tiefling make eye contact.

She feels her forehead furrow again before she can stop it and immediately floods calm across her features. Her brows spring back into place a little too quickly, and she feels that too, a frustrated flush rising along her cheekbones. *Dammit, Dog.*

The tiefling quirks a brow of their own. Lora rolls her eyes and looks away.

When she glances back, they're still watching her over the rim of their mug.

Lora lets her eyes narrow as she gives them a slow, thorough once-over. The tiefling sips from their drink, unconcerned by the scrutiny.

They are, Lora's impartial assessment concludes, hot as fuck.

Also, she's staring.

She watches them brush a few stray curls out of their eyes, thumb lingering a bit too long at the base of one mahogany horn, circling one spot in a casual gesture that could be mistaken for merely scratching an itch. Are they *modeling* for her?

The dog wriggles out from where she buried it, gnawing on the single thought **(FRIEND?)** like a particularly captivating stick. Lora squashes it back down, flips open the menu, and busies herself with it until the waitress comes around.

"I'm Asha," the waitress introduces herself. "And *you've* got an admirer."

Lora's eyes dart to the tiefling, and Asha nods.

"He's a regular, when he's in town," she goes on. "Tips respectfully. Always polite. Never too drunk. Chatty, but none of us know a thing about his personal life, which seems by design. Want me to tell him to fuck off?"

Lora blinks, tips her head, and remembers how to form human speech. "No. I think we're good."

Asha nods again. "If that changes, you can let any of us know. Can I get you anything to drink?"

The few coins in Lora's pocket press against her leg, and she hesitates.

"Don't worry." Asha brushes her reluctance away. "The first one's on him, and whatever he does for work pays *really* well."

"Are you sure?" Lora asks, and she feels the girl's eyes run over her.

We must look a mess, Lora worries. She hasn't looked at her human self in a mirror for days, and the last puddle she saw Dog reflected in revealed half as much mud as fur. From the back of their head, Dog lets out a low-pitched whine. *She'd have every right to kick us out, or tell someone to have us arrested for vagrancy.*

The waitress's tone is softer with her next words. "Treat yourself, love. He's good for the coin, and you look like you could use it."

Lora finds herself nodding, swallowing down an unexpected lump in her throat. *If I were a wolf—*

But she isn't a wolf. Right now, she's not even a dog, and her human vocal cords aren't made for howling.

Instead, she orders a warm milk beverage that promises notes of bergamot, strawberry, violet, and honey.

"And a muffin," Lora adds on a whim, while the

waitress nods and writes it all down. "And maybe bring it to his table? If I'm over there."

She waits for Asha to question her, to slide across the bench and grill her like one of Lora's cousins would, but the waitress only nods, repeats the order back, and disappears into the kitchen, leaving Lora alone at her table again.

She spends a moment collecting her thoughts and suppressing the instinct to run, then hauls herself up and across the room.

The tiefling pretends not to watch her approach and only looks up from his notebook as Lora stops at the table.

"Drinking alone?" she asks.

He quirks an eyebrow. "Not if you're planning to join me."

Lora gives him a moment of side-eye before sliding into the vacant seat. "I appreciate the drink."

"I appreciate the company," the tiefling replies with an easy smile. "Tobias Macauley. He and him pronouns."

"Lora," she responds. "She. What are you drinking?"

"Coffee." Tobias shrugs. *(Black)*—the dog informs her. "Long night ahead."

"Work or fun?"

Lora hadn't meant it *like that*, but the boy's startled

laugh is genuine.

"I… suppose I'm flexible," he replies, and Lora's ears heat.

Mercifully, Tobias goes on, "I leave town tomorrow, so any fun has to be short lived. As for the long night, I haven't been sleeping well lately, so I thought I'd commit to being awake. Get some reading done, the like."

"Well," Lora ventures, the knot in her chest loosening slightly, "If you're drinking *that* every day as the sun goes down, I might have an idea as to why you haven't been sleeping."

Tobias's grin spreads. "Do you hand out sleeping advice to everyone who buys you a drink?"

"No." Lora shrugs, opting for honesty. "But then, no one's ever bought me a drink before."

"Well, I'm glad I could set that right," Tobias declares. "And I'd be glad to buy you another."

Lora laughs, leaning back in the seat. "Don't go buying drinks before I've drunk them. You don't even know about the muffin."

"A muffin? No! Gods!" Tobias gasps, clutching his chest. "My finances are in tatters. You've destroyed me in one blow."

"I—" *could destroy you with another one.*

Lora cuts the joke off so fast she bites her tongue in

the process, and the dog whines and wiggles on the floor of her mind, restless energy rolling off of it in waves. "Ow, *fuck*!"

"Are you alright?" Tobias asks, but Lora is spared from answering by the server's perfectly timed return.

"One coffee refill," Asha announces as Lora brushes off Tobias's concern. "One Lady Firefly, and one apple maple muffin."

"If the muffin is too much—" Lora begins, but Tobias dismisses the rest with a wave.

"Lora, right? I promise you, I do not give a single fuck about the muffin. Are you well?"

Tobias fixes her in his gaze, the intensity startling, and Lora's flush blooms into a forest fire.

"Bit my tongue," she mumbles, searching for anything else to settle her attention on. "That's all."

Her drink has come in a ceramic mug, glazed in the tavern's signature dark blue, with speckles of purples, blues, oranges, golds, and greens. It does resemble a night field full of lightning bugs, and the stoneware warms her hands as Lora distracts herself with several long sips.

Tobias must have picked up on her unease because he's returned to lightly sketching by the time she looks back up. Without thinking, Lora cranes her neck to see, and Tobias quickly turns the page, beginning to write in a scrawl so unreadable it may as well be code.

Lora decides to take a different approach. "Who does your tattoos?"

She couldn't see the details from across the room, but up close, they're striking. Tobias's throat, in particular, is covered by a sleeve of small, intricate markings done in a variety of shimmering inks that give the same effect as pigeon feathers. If the marks are writing, the language is foreign to Lora, but they start at Tobias's clavicle and climb upwards until they disappear behind his ears.

"Oh," Tobias passes a hand over the markings. "Just a family friend. Can't remember the name of the shop. They've changed it a couple of times."

"They look like—" Lora's mouth is full of muffin, and she cuts one index finger through the air in a zig-zag pattern instead.

"Sound waves?" Tobias grins. "Good. That was the intent. Nerd shit, I know."

"They're cool," Lora insists. "*Very* on theme for a mysterious tavern frequenter."

"Alright, alright," Tobias deflects, laughing good-naturedly. "My turn to ask the questions. Why are you in town? Besides free drinks"— Lora squawks in protest — "*and* muffins, and sleep advice?"

"How do you know I'm not from here?" Lora counters, and Tobias shakes his head.

"Nobody's *from* Glenhurst," he explains. "It's a waypoint. More inns than houses; no schools for children."

Lora hadn't noticed that.

"And sure," Tobias goes on, "There's folks who live here, and folks who pass through regularly. But if you lived here, you'd work somewhere, and if you were a regular, I'd have seen you around."

"You'd bet your dignity on that?" Lora teases.

"In a heartbeat," Tobias says with a motion over his heart. "Besides, I'm good with faces."

He leans closer, and the howling in Lora's ears swells to a crescendo. "And I *certainly* wouldn't forget yours."

Flustered, Lora responds by stuffing a bite of muffin in her mouth, making an elaborate show of taking her time and holding up a finger for Tobias to wait until she's finished. Inside, the dog has its teeth in (**FRIEND?**) and is shaking it like a pillow.

"I'm… traveling." It's the best she can come up with, once the pretense of chewing her food has been exhausted. Sprinkling a little truth into her story seems safest. "Had to get out of my hometown, so I'm looking for a job, I guess? Or something."

Tobias nods sympathetically. "The post office bulletin board is the best place for job postings. Steady, seasonal, and gig work—all there."

Lora tips her head in acknowledgment. "Any suggestions for something else?"

"Ah," Tobias hums. "Pleasure, rather than work?"

Lora shrugs, raising her eyebrows at him.

Tobias glances out the window, where a soft rain is beginning to fall. "You have somewhere dry to stay tonight, right?"

"What?" Lora follows his gaze, confused by the sudden change in subject. "Oh, *fuck me*."

That startles another laugh out of Tobias, bright and clear. "I thought we were at least a few more witty banters from that part of the evening, but yeah, if you want."

"I—I mean—" Lora blushes, warmth blooming in her chest. "You're leaving in the morning."

Tobias glances down at his mug, the refill already drained again. "Oh, horrors. My aspirations of spending the whole night in deep—albeit highly caffeinated— slumber have been absolutely shredded."

His tone is as dry as the bottom of the mug, and Lora snorts out a laugh.

"I supposed you weren't very subtle about that," she agrees.

"I mean," Tobias goes on, folding his notebook shut and stuffing it in the pocket of his coat. "I'm happy to buy another round of drinks first. I'm staying just upstairs. Haven't tested the theory, but the bed seems big enough for two."

A hopeful half-smile tugs on the corner of his mouth, and the dog inside of Lora rolls across the floor and howls.

Distractions, Lora thinks. *New experiences.*

(ANYTHING BESIDES SITTING STILL FOR ANOTHER HOURRRRRRR.)

"Alright," Lora decides, leaning her elbows against the table.

Tobias mirrors her pose, and suddenly their faces are inches away. He smells like anise, coffee, cumin, and something sharp and acrid besides.

Silver.

Fire.

Magic.

Lora could gladly let herself drown in an ocean of his scent. She wonders idly what she smells like before circling back to the issue at hand.

"Nothing serious," she informs him.

Tobias shakes his head. "Absolutely not."

"If either of us says stop, the whole thing's off."

His eyes are deadly serious. "Of course."

Lora sniffs. "Are you wearing jewelry?"

"Are you robbing me?" Tobias laughs, but his gaze has sharpened, and he regards her with interest.

Lora chews at her lip. "Metal allergy."

Tobias eyes her for a moment more before acquiescing with a shrug. "Three ear piercings, all bronze. Silver cuff, left ear—my left. A couple of iron and silver rings."

Lora sniffs the air again, her brow furrowing.

"Knife in my boot," he adds curiously. "Iron, silver edges."

Lora nods once. "Lose the silver, throw in breakfast."

"Mmm," Tobias hums, leaning closer. "You drive a hard bargain."

Lora wiggles her eyebrows suggestively, and Tobias laughs.

"Shit outta luck if you're looking for that equipment," he admits conspiratorially. "But I did take classes to be a sculptor a few years back."

Lora cocks her head, and Tobias breaks into a toothy grin.

"I got really good with my hands."

Her groan only makes him laugh harder. After catching his breath, he sticks out his hand.

"To reiterate: no silver, over by morning; breakfast on me? At-will agreement, further verbal amendments treated as binding."

Lora slides her hand into his, and they shake.

"Actual binding negotiable?" she asks, eliciting another laugh from Tobias.

"Actual binding negotiable."

"Well then," Lora says, draining the last of her drink and pulling Tobias to his feet, "What the hell are we waiting for?"

CHAPTER 2

On a different side of Glenhurst, a lone figure trudges through the drizzle, head down, one wing raised in an attempt to shield the rest of their body from the worst of the rain. In the early twilight, the street lamps catch and glimmer in stray strands of their hair, highlighting subtle notes of blue and pink and gold.

Nicodemus Miles left his horse at the stables by the town gates, reasoning that at least one of them deserved to stay warm and dry tonight, but now he's starting to regret not doubling back and crashing on the floor of his horse's stall.

Lost in dreams of warmth, dry clothes, and the smell of hay and horse breath, Nic startles as a window above his head slams open, and a child's voice hollers down.

"'Scuse me, mister! Are you an angel?"

Nic barely keeps from cursing, face burning despite

the chill in the air as vague noises of disapproval waft down from the same direction as the shouting.

Nic has been on the receiving end of enough scoldings to understand the shape of it.

Don't yell out the window.

Don't stick your head out in the rain.

Don't watch people on the street when it's bedtime.

Don't ask strangers personal questions.

The cardinal rules of childhood. Nic's were different, but he *is* familiar with the concept of normal rules.

He set out from home thinking winged folk were as common in the rest of the world as they were in his small town. That belief was quickly disproved by the third town full of stares and second looks.

He's lucky that Beau and his family—for all their many faults—didn't bat an eye at his wings and color-shifting hair, or a younger Nic might've turned around and ended his quest before it had hardly begun.

The children are the worst offenders, despite their intentions being more innocent than most. He's been called a bird, harpy, and his least favorite—an angel.

Nic doesn't feel like an angel. Right now, he feels like a piece of chewed gum stuck to the heel of a cursed pair of boots.

As if to emphasize the *cursed* bit, the rain picks up,

darting through the open front of his cloak. Cursing again, Nic pulls it tighter with one hand, the other curled tightly around the scribbled address on his palm, tucked safely out of the elements. The feathers on his wings ruffle in protest against the wind, and he breaks into an awkward half-run, travel bag pounding against his leg.

He hopes the contact he's supposed to be meeting is home. They're not anyone he knows personally but rather a connection that his sister Arleth made at school.

"You might find them... a little unconventional," he remembers Ari warning him, with an uncharacteristic hesitance in her voice. "But hear him out."

Nic laughed, at the time. "Unconventional? I've survived your batshit inventions for years. I think I can handle a couple of quirks."

The topic moved on after Ari hit him in the forehead with her crumpled up breakfast napkin. Ari's one of the smartest people Nic knows, and if she says someone knows their shit, he's inclined to trust her. Besides, the months before that had gotten him nothing but dead ends, and although he's always been loath to give anything up, Nic was starting to consider quitting.

He still might, if this person doesn't have anything for him. Ari's visit was a stroke of luck, and Nic's not sure he has another backup plan, except to head back to the Tayag family with his wings hung low in shame.

Across the street, a tarnished number 7 hangs cocked,

catching his eye, and Nic bolts in its direction. He doesn't see the puddle at the bottom of the stairs and swears again as his foot lands squarely in it, thoroughly soaking his pants up to the knee.

The rain has emptied the streets, driving citizens indoors and ridding Nic of any instinct he may have had for stealth. His boots drum a rhythm of exhaustion up the porch steps, and he knocks heavily on the door with his fist. Spotting a bell, Nic prompts several piercing peals from that as well.

The house remains silent, and the windows stay dark.

Nic rings the bell again.

This time, the curtain of a second-floor window drifts to one side, and Nic catches a flicker of blue light behind it.

"Hey!" Nic shoots one hand into the air, waving it wildly back and forth.

The curtain falls back into place.

"Come *on*," Nic groans and yanks sharply on the bell again.

It comes off in his hand.

Nic stares at it, his brain cycling through excuses as the breeze changes directions and rain begins to patter against his back again. He can hear footsteps from inside now, and the rattling of a deadbolt being undone.

Nic barely has the presence of mind to stuff his hand, doorbell and all, inside the pocket of his cloak before the door swings open.

The person staring out at him is about Nic's own age, with hair the color of riverbed silt and a furrowed brow that doesn't bode well for Nic's prospects of getting out of the rain.

Nic tries anyway. "Artham?"

The furrow deepens further. "Who are you?"

"I—" Nic flounders. "My sister went to school with a friend of yours—Cynthi? She probably told you I was coming tomorrow, but I made good time, and—"

The stranger's face is clearing already, and they dive out of the way, swinging the door open wide behind them. "Oh! Gods, sorry! Come in, it's horrid out."

Nic takes a second to shake the excess *wet* from his wings before ducking inside as well. "I'm sorry. I know I'm a day earlier than I planned."

"No! Gods, no need to apologize. I wouldn't have been ready then either, in all likelihood. I lost track of the days this week, and I'm"—a ghost of an unreadable emotion crosses their face—"not very good friends with time."

"You *are* Artham though, right?" Nic confirms, and the stranger nods, sticking out a hand.

"Art, yeah. My grams—my, uh, grandmothers—don't

even call me Artham. That's the other thing that threw me off. And you're…?"

Art trails off, grimacing apologetically.

"Nic." His cloak is half off, making Nic acutely aware of the way his rain-speckled shirt hugs in uncomfortable places. "He pronouns. Yours?"

Art shrugs. "He, they, whatever. What's that saying? Don't care what you call me as long as you're not yelling it?"

Nic blinks. "Is that a regional expression?"

His host gives another shrug. "A boy I dated used to say something like it. Might've picked it up from him."

Nic nods slowly, and Art gestures to his coat. "Want me to take that?"

Fuck. I still have his doorbell in my pocket.

"Sure."

Nic passes them the coat, and the other boy disappears through a door with it, leaving their guest to size up the room.

The primary piece of furniture in the room is an old sofa, a worn-out shade of green approaching olive, and Nic perches himself on the arm of it. More than one cushion is speckled with paint stains, and several are heavily patched, the mending done in fabrics of varying colors and mis-matched prints.

The house is wood, and its walls are bare, save for a few gauzey curtains, hung over the windows in a pretense of privacy. A couple of black bookcases hold shelves of notebooks and novels in varying conditions. Nic doesn't recognize most of the titles, but he gets the impression that they would fall closer to his sister's reading tastes than his. Of the two of them, she's always preferred tales of magic and speculation.

"Are you hungry?" Art calls from the adjoining room, and Nic considers the question.

"I could eat," he responds, hauling himself off the couch as he hears the rattling of cupboards and utensils begin in earnest.

"Oh, good," Art says as Nic enters the kitchen. "I haven't properly cooked for someone in ages."

"I don't need anything special," Nic starts to protest, but Art waves his concern away, already filling the counter with more vegetables than Nic's eaten since he left the Tayags' farm behind. "Do you want my help?"

Art shrugs again. "Can if you want. No debts, no obligations."

Nic opts for "no obligations" and finds a seat for himself on one of the refurbished barstools that serve as kitchen seating.

"Where's your accent from?" he finds himself asking, curiosity overwhelming his usual leanings toward politeness and decorum. "My sister said your family was from Addersford."

Art's back is to Nic, but he can still hear his host's hands stutter, splashing water over the edge of the pot he's rinsing; the soft *"gods-fuck"* as Art swipes a towel down the front of his shirt.

"Oh, you know," Art answers, his back still to Nic, "Here and there."

Nic doesn't know, but he can tell a brush off when one's directed at him.

"So," Art continues as if nothing has happened, tossing the hand towel over the back of a chair and resuming his cooking prep, "I heard you're looking for some sort of magical item?"

Nic lets out a sigh, leaning his elbows on the stool's backrest. "Yeah, kind of. I'm pretty sure it's a knife."

Art nods, clearly waiting for Nic to continue. Nic does not.

"Just, like, any knife?" Art clarifies after a moment of silence has elapsed.

"Well, no. It is a specific knife—or probably a knife. Definitely a specific object. Which the evidence seems to imply is… knife-shaped, at least?"

Art twists around to pin Nic with a skeptical look. "And Cynthi sent you to *me*?"

Nic sighs again, running a hand through his hair. He spent the whole ride to Glenhurst practicing this conversation, although his horse had asked significantly less questions.

"What's your stance on prophecies?" Nic finally asks.

"Fuck 'em," Art responds immediately, turning back to the stove.

The rice has begun to boil, a steady undercurrent of sound that joins with the wind and rain outside. Nic waits for a minute, but Art doesn't seem like he plans to elaborate.

Nic tries again. "I mean, whether they're real or not."

"Does it matter?" Art asks, slicing up celery. "Following them seems to lead more people wrong than it steers right."

"*I'm* following one." Nic says, frowning. "There's a wizard killing everything that grows within half a day of his tower, and the families living on that land can't last much longer without their crops."

"Sounds like an asshole with magic, not a prophecy," Art remarks.

"Sure," Nic acquiesces reluctantly. "But my fiance is counting on me, and if this wizard is being propped up by something big enough to kill miles and miles of land, I want to have a little more up my sleeve than a family sword before I face him."

His dry tone elicits the intended laugh from Art, who's begun mixing up a heavenly-smelling combination of spices. Nic takes the laughter as a sign to keep going.

"I did some research. My sister's a sorcerer, so she pointed me towards some books on *relevant relics* and *pertinent portents* for *the times we're in now*. When I found some lore about a magical blade that could heal a land of malice and drought, I thought it sounded... applicable."

Nic still thinks it sounds more than applicable, but the excitement that had seized his heart upon discovery feels... silly? Shameful, perhaps? Whatever the emotion, it doesn't feel like it belongs here, miles away, in the kitchen of a stranger, sharing the same air with the aromatics Art is currently sauteing.

This is Nic's most solid lead, and now is a time for persuasive arguments, not foolish, swayable things like *hope*.

"Alright, man." Art sighs. "How do I fit into things?"

"My sister knows a bunch of people from school, so she did some asking around on my behalf. Her friend Cynthi said she knew a guy who knew a lot about...." Nic hesitates, once again on rocky footing. "Killing wizards? Or area of effect spells, maybe? I couldn't get all the information quite in order, but she said you might be worth talking to. I was kind of hoping you'd be able to tell me."

That feels as good a point as any to stop talking, so Nic does. His back feels like cardboard, folded in half along the spine, and Nic crowds the tension out of his shoulders, filling them with calm until there's no space left for worry. He wraps his legs around the legs of the stool, and keeps his breathing even. Aside from the occasional twitch of his wings, he's excised all his anxious tells. His wings might tip off a stubborn observer, but Art is cooking, and Nic is well versed in dismissing questions about his well-being.

It'll be okay, he promises himself, one thumb running in small circles against his other wrist. *There's a plan. I've got a plan.*

Art, for his part, seems to be thinking about how to respond, and after a few minutes pass in pregnant silence, Nic settles in for the wait.

Outside, the storm is raging. Thunder crackles, and Lora cuddles deeper against the furnace of Tobias's chest, glad for its warmth. Tobias makes a sleepy noise and kisses her forehead.

They've both lost their shirts, and Lora watches the scars under Tobias's pecs rise and fall with his breaths. He's inked over them, another tangle in the tapestry of art he wears on his skin. On the left, a *V* of geese takes flight, heading in the direction of his armpit and leaving a tangle of rosebush thorns behind them. His heartbeat is fast, and Lora's foot drums against the bedsheets, echoing its rhythm under the covers.

Tobias follows her gaze, interlacing his fingers with hers.

"My first girlfriend," he explains softly. "We were two trans ships, passing in the night, each headed where the other had been. We were killing time in the same school, and joked that we might as well trade genders for something to do."

"You got your gender secondhand?" Lora laughs. "What would you have done if she didn't want your first one? Donated it to the school thrift store?"

"Of course not." Tobias grins. "That shit was mint condition. I'd bring it to the closest Night Market."

"Oh, sure," Lora teases, pushing herself up on one elbow. "That sounds like a wise decision."

"Wise decisions are my least favorite kind," Tobias teases back, rolling his eyes. "But you're right. As it was, I got ripped off. All the same shit in masc, *and* I had to restart puberty."

Lora laughs, but Tobias goes quiet, running a thumb along his scars.

More thunder rumbles in the distance, and a breeze snakes through the drafty walls, making the flames of the bedside candles dance.

"Do you miss her?" Lora asks, after a moment.

Tobias lets out a soft laugh.

"Her name was Swan, *like the goose,*" he quotes, avoiding the question. "She insisted. I haven't seen her in… probably ten years now."

Lora lets out a low whistle, and Tobias shakes his head, tugging her against his side again. Lora obliges, nestling back into the crook of his arm.

"She was a satyr raised by fauns," Tobias muses, before catching himself. "And you definitely didn't go to all the trouble of fucking me just to unearth all my sad ex stories."

"Trouble?" Lora scoffs. "You were begging me a minute ago."

Tobias cackles, and Lora grins, nipping at his arm. He settles one arm around her waist, grazing her side with a touch that makes something leap in Lora's gut.

"Fuck you," she gasps, struggling to breathe normally again.

Tobias grins. "You already did that."

Lora wriggles around, and a shudder passes through Tobias's body as her mouth grazes his ear. "I'll do it again."

Tobias's hands slide upwards, snarling in her curls,

and Lora kisses him, long and slow, until he pulls away for breath.

"You're going to make me beg again," Tobias moans, though he doesn't sound entirely displeased at the prospect. "Is that your plan?"

"If I told you that," Lora whispers against his lips. "I'd have to kill you."

"You could kill me," Tobias murmurs, closing the gap to kiss her hungrily. "I'd let you."

Lora laughs, rocking back on her heels. "What about your job? In the morning?"

"The night is still young," Tobias pouts, pulling Lora closer again. "The good die young, and the old live long enough to write people out of their wills."

"Their fault for having wills," Lora hums, reveling in the scent of Tobias's curls. "Who even has those?"

"I do," Tobias protests, laughing as he flips her over on the bed. "You don't?"

"Mm-nm," Lora shakes her head against the pillow, hair spreading out beneath her like a cloud. "I've got *better* things to do with my time."

Tobias takes the hint, and time blurs into a delightful haze once more.

— - ◆ ✧ ◆ - ✦ ✳ ✦ - ◆ ✧ ◆ - —

Art keeps Nic waiting on his answer for a while. The kitchen stays quiet, aside from the sounds of the fire, the rain, and a few faint threads of music coming from… well, somewhere. Nic is pretty sure he's narrowed it down to a strange-looking box, glowing from a glass orb in the center of a wood, mesh, and wire shell.

Art has been quiet for so long that Nic has taken to counting in his head, a childhood pattern that he hasn't yet been able to shake.

He's passing 600 and about to start again when Art kills the cooking flames, deposits the knife and cutting board unceremoniously in the sink, and offers his guest an empty plate, gesturing to the stove.

"You can serve yourself. Don't worry about saving leftovers, if you're hungry enough to finish any of it."

Nic scrambles down from the chair, accepting the plate and heading for the stove.

"The rice is just plain," Art explains. "All the meat is contained to the big pan—chicken, squash, your general aromatics—minus garlic, so onion and celery. That's all seasoned with a little bit of coriander, turmeric, cilantro, poppy seeds, and lemon. The smaller pan has diced cauliflower, apple, pine nuts, more celery, dried onion, and a ginger paste with sunflower oil that I'm trying out."

"Shit," Nic whistles. "Do I mix them?"

Art shrugs, idling in the doorway. "Can if you want. You know what you like better than I do, but they should complement each other."

Nic fills his plate with three neat, separate piles of food and follows the other boy back into the living room. Art tosses a spare cushion onto the floor, arranging himself on it so that he can rest his back against the wall, and Nic resumes his perch on the couch.

Art waits until Nic has taken a couple of bites and then breathes deeply, setting his plate to the side.

"So," he begins, with the air of someone embarking on a familiar course, "Cynthi either sent you to me for help, or for *the talk*. You're getting the talk either way, and then you can decide if you want the help."

"I do—" Nic assures him earnestly, but Art holds up a hand.

"Just listen, for a second," he says.

Nic is struck suddenly by how tired Art looks. Earlier, Nic had guessed him to be barely on the other side of twenty-one, Nic's own age. Now he wonders if he might have drastically undershot.

"I meant what I said about prophecies," Art goes on. "Doesn't matter if they're real or not. Doesn't matter if they work or not. Anything that wants to shape your life without living it first is absolutely not something you can put your full faith in. Understand? If you want to use some dead person's poetry or predictions to help you feel better about whatever you've got to do, do it. But make sure *you're* the one using *it*. They're tools, not trades."

Nic frowns but keeps his mouth shut. Art continues.

"Second"—he pauses, and Nic looks up from his food to find Art leaning forward, their eyes boring into his—"and I know this is a personal question, so forgive me. Have you killed anyone before?"

Nic's heart lurches. *Fire. Dragon breath. Every eye in the town on him.*

The truth ekes out in a coarse whisper. "No."

Art nods. There's no judgment on his face, just a deep sadness.

"Wouldn't advise it," he says softly. "Obviously, we all do what we have to. I can tell you're not taking this shit lightly, but if you're planning to show up at this man's house with a knife, or sword, or whatever—anything sharp enough to do some damage—be sure you're damn ready to finish the job with it."

Nic looks away, busying himself with another bite of food. He barely tastes it, mouth full of sidewalk dust and copper between his teeth.

"Anything else?" he manages.

Art sighs, resting his shoulders back against the wall. "I don't know where to find your knife, but I've got some connections in the local artificer scene and a couple of scholars who I can reach out to about relics of magical significance."

"That would be incredible," Nic breathes.

Art goes on. "I've got an appointment tomorrow morning for a job I'm thinking of taking. The pay is more than enough to cover next month's rent, and I could use the windfall. It might take a week, but it'd go faster with two of us. If you want to team up, we can split the pay. I'd rather work with someone I already trust, as opposed to a stranger, and if all goes well, I'll have a bit of time to help you with your thing before I've gotta worry about work again."

"You trust me?" Nic asks, caught off guard.

Art shrugs. "Are you going to give me a reason I shouldn't?"

Nic hesitates.

I freeze up. I let people down. I've had one job in my life, and I couldn't even do that.

Art waits patiently.

"What kind of job?" Nic asks instead, biting back the other words.

"I'll find out tomorrow," Art says. "These kinds of ads are usually vague, either to keep the employers' hand close to their chest or to make sure they don't attract the wrong folks for the wrong reasons. They're high risk, high reward, but this one is being billed as a community service, and there's some legitimate names backing it. Pockets deep enough to make good on their promises."

Nic catches himself chewing on his lip and rubs at his nose to cover for it while he thinks. It'll mean more time away from the farm, from Beau. On the other hand, if Art really can help, it'll also mean less time chasing his own tail, trying to figure out leads on his own.

Nic looks back up at Art. He's made his choice.

"You'll have a place to stay in town, either way," the other boy assures him.

Nic nods solemnly. "I'm in."

"Perfect." Art cracks a half smile and hauls himself to his feet. "You can sleep on the couch. The cushions come off, and—I'll show you in a minute. You're done eating?"

Nic ferries the last remnants of food from his plate to his mouth and bobs his head in assent while he chews.

"I can help with dishes," he mumbles.

"Awesome." Art lights up. "Oh! I almost forgot. How was the food?"

$\mathcal{C}$HAPTER 3

"You've *really* never thought about what to put in your will?" Tobias presses over breakfast in the morning, shoveling a forkful of pancakes in his mouth and regarding Lora doubtfully.

Lora groans, casting her hands wide in exasperation. This is the third time Tobias has circled back around to their innocent pillow talk conversation, and Lora is running out of things to say on the subject. "Literally not a single time."

Tobias's brow scrunches. "Because *you don't have one*."

"Correct. I do not have an elaborate secret will that I'm exclusively lying to you about." Lora rolls her eyes. "If I die, my family can figure out what to do with my shit. I don't have anything worth fighting over, anyways."

She pauses in the middle of mopping up excess syrup from her plate, pointing the end of her fork—saturated pancake and all—at Tobias. "Wait. Do *you* have a will?"

Tobias gestures to his conveniently full mouth, and Lora narrows her eyes, making it clear that she plans to wait for the answer. After a minute of chewing, Tobias reaches for his coffee, but Lora snatches it away.

"Answer me," she orders, taking a demure sip from Tobias's mug and ignoring his indignant spluttering. "Or else you'll be drinking *water* until it's time to hit the road."

Tobias scowls. "I could order another, you know."

"You absolutely could not," Lora laughs. "The server is a total girls' girl. She actually told me to rip you off last night, did you know that? Now tell me about your will, or you're cut off."

"Unbelievable," Tobias grumbles. "I gave up the bonds of sisterhood for what, slutty v-neck shirts?"

Lora barely keeps the coffee in her mouth and not spewed across the table. The idea of Tobias in a low-cut shirt, loose fitting perhaps, and tailored to accentuate his waist…

Despite the fact that she saw him in much less last night, it's distracting at best.

One look at the devilish grin on Tobias's face

confirms that the joke has garnered exactly the reaction he intended.

Lora matches his scowl, and the boy rolls his eyes, holding up both hands in surrender. "Alright, yes, I yield! Obviously I have a will. I wrote my first one when I was… twelve? Something like that. I update it every two seasons or so."

Lora is so preoccupied with gaping at him that she forgets to hand the coffee back until he plucks it from her hand, raising it in a jaunty toast before downing the remaining quarter of a cup. "*Twice* a *year*?"

"What?" Tobias blinks. "Oh—tax seasons. Every four years."

"*Every four years*." Lora repeats.

Tobias frowns. "It's an important document to keep current."

Lora runs a hand through her hair, still staring at Tobias. Her breakfast has been forgone in the pursuit of tastier gossip.

"What could even be in it?"

"Dispersal of assets, disposal of remains," Tobias lists. "Various vengeance and retribution clauses. Transference of debts, resurrection exemptions—"

Lora blinks a couple of times. "What the *fuck* did you say you did for work again?"

It's the wrong question, and Lora feels the aftershocks of it like a chill, sweeping through their banter. Tobias doesn't miss a beat, but she watches a wall descend behind his eyes.

"I didn't," Tobias answers, glancing out the window. "I do a lot of things. Today, I'll be getting on a horse and riding through likely abominable weather conditions until I reconsider leaving my home for the foreseeable future."

Lora opens her mouth to respond, grasping for a clever retort that will return things to the way they've been, but her one night stand is already pulling several bills from a wallet he's conjured out of thin air.

Large bills, Lora observes, with a minor amount of shock.

(Smells like smoke) Dog contributes, snuffling in her ear. *(Gross smoke.)*

Tobias slings his bag over one shoulder and slides from the booth, tucking the cash under the edge of his plate.

When did he stack his cup and silverware on top?

How long has he been preparing to exit?

He places a hand on Lora's shoulder, and she blinks up at him, still trying to catch up.

"Thank you for the fun," Tobias says, and it sounds genuine, but something in his touch itches strangely against Lora's skin. "I'll remind you that we agreed against forming any lasting connections. Regardless, I do wish you all the best in your endeavors, and should we ever find ourselves across the bar from one another again, it might be fun to catch up."

His hand disappears, and by the time Lora has twisted around to follow his exit with her eyes, Tobias has passed through the door without a single glance back.

Art wakes with the dawn, if he slept at all.

Drifting in and out of sleep on an unfamiliar couch, Nic hears him make his way downstairs in the dark, cross the living room, and enter the kitchen, where he starts to cook.

Nic is pretty sure the other boy is trying to be quiet, but it doesn't seem to be the kind of thing that comes naturally to him, if the tandem sounds of clattering and cursing from the kitchen are anything to go by.

Eventually, Nic gives up on the potential for any more sleep, shambling into the kitchen and waving away Art's sheepish apologies.

"'s my own damn fault," he mumbles. "Usually I have stuff to block out noise with, but I left them in a jacket and lost them in the river the last time I tried to wash it."

"I wish I'd known last night." Art shakes his head.

"I've got a couple of spares in the bathroom for friends. You're welcome to a set."

Nic starts to protest, but Art counters it immediately.

"Look, it'll be easier for me to replace a spare set in my own town than it would be for you to find a new pair in an unfamiliar place. You've got better things to spend your coin on. Eggs?"

The eggs are delicious, and Art chatters the whole time about the local—and apparently thriving—community aid network where he sources most of his produce.

"The lady who started it is incredible," Art gushes as they clean, pack up, and head out to the meeting. "Actually, she might be a good lead for your thing. I think one of her almost-siblings is a specialty blacksmith."

"Almost-sibling?" Nic echoes.

"Oh yeah." Art nods. "Their dad's a bastard, from what I hear, so he got disowned."

"Oh. I'm sorry."

"No, no," Art rushes to correct himself. "They both disowned their dad. And they weren't raised together, so they felt weird calling themselves sibling and sister. It's a whole inside thing, you know?"

Nic does not know, but he decides it's not an avenue worth pursuing.

After breakfast, Lora makes her way to the post office.

From experience, she knows that most buildings in Glenhurst don't allow animals inside of them—not unaccompanied, at least. A reasonable ruling, even if it does provoke Dog to fill their head with angry barking as their human form passes by the sign without issue.

Lora locates the job board easily but finds herself stuck, once face-to-face with the object of her desire.

What kind of job will make her family proud? What kind of accomplishment will make them forget their disappointment?

Seventy-nine years of successful ceremonies, Lora thinks, nails digging crescent-shaped indentations into her palms. *Why did mine have to go wrong?*

Dog growls and barks, but Lora can hear the traces of a whimper underneath his noise.

It did go wrong. You are not a wolf.

Dog slinks into a corner to sulk.

In the end, Lora picks a job at random and, with the wind skating shivers across her fur-less arms, sets out to reshape her destiny.

It's a short walk to the library, which Nic and Art pass in companionable silence. When they reach their destination, Art holds the door open, and Nic gets his first proper look at the Glenhurst Common Library.

It's a small building, but the space is utilized well. Shelving covers the walls from floor to ceiling, and a number of stools are scattered intermittently about. A neat little basket sits on the edge of the reference desk with a stack of paper slips inside.

A sign reads *For Things in High Places (Single-Use Levitation Spells),* and several flyers are pasted about with instructions on how to charge and cast.

The main room is brightly furnished, if a little worn and well-loved, and a young librarian in a wheelchair looks up, smiling at them as they enter.

"That's Gaia," Art tells Nic, waving. "We'll want to talk to her when we get back."

Nic's eyes snag on a small, delicately stitched tag sewn to the sleeve of Gaia's dark jacket. He can read the text if he squints.

she ~ zer ~ they

Pronouns, he realizes, and feels something hot and jealous seize in his chest.

Art blows the librarian a kiss, and they laugh and flip him off as he drags Nic deeper into the rows of shelves.

There are tables beyond the shelves, Nic realizes. Art

guides them to one in particular, where two people are already seated. The older of the two, a blonde-haired man with a full beard and expensive-looking jacket, glances up as they approach—and frowns. His younger companion twists around in her chair, following the man's gaze.

"Artham," the man grunts, sounding displeased though not openly hostile. Art flashes him a polite smile. "I thought you might turn up."

"Yessir," Art replies. "My friend and I are here about the job posting."

The man turns his gaze to Nic, who resists the sudden urge to squirm.

He extends his hand instead. "Nic Miles, sir."

"Jacob Lantlit," the man responds dourly, shaking Nic's hand. "I'm afraid someone's beat you boys to the punch."

Nic looks to the girl, who definitely squirms under his appraisal.

"I don't mind sharing," she says quickly. "More hands, more heads."

Lantlit huffs. "The payment is non-negotiable, you understand. You'll have to work out a split between yourselves."

"Of course," Art says smoothly, flashing another disarming smile. "We're all professionals here."

Lantlit snorts.

"As I've already told Miss Abernathy," he says, passing them a second and third copy of the folder that the girl is already holding, "there's been a string of disappearances in the stretch of taiga between here and Baslam. Missing persons aside, it's causing a significant trade disruption."

Art nods sagely. "Everybody loves a shortcut."

"Unfortunately so," Lantlit hums. "All the information we have is in those folders. You'll be the third crew we've sent out there."

"The others were unsuccessful?" the girl asks, looking up.

Lantlit purses his lips. "The whereabouts of the others cannot currently be confirmed."

Art sobers, and Nic lets out a low whistle. Lantlit fixes them both with a stern look.

"It's not a task for children," he says tersely, and Art's expression clouds over.

"But," their would-be employer grits his teeth and goes on, "Mr. Gothard, I know your qualifications as well as anyone else around here. The listing has been up long enough for us to lose two more supply runs, and with you three as the only interested parties, we're just about out of options."

"Why can't you send in the Guard?" Art asks.

"Because"—Lantlit looks like he had tasted something sour—"I've been informed that we can't afford to waste valuable manpower on an unknown threat. This is a matter for adventurers. You're…"

An uncomfortable pause stretches between them.

"Uniquely qualified," the man finishes.

Nic's pretty sure that all of them heard the word he didn't say. *Disposable.*

"You'll discover the source of the disappearances and alert a response unit via sending stone," their patron goes on, sliding a smooth, round stone with a hole in the middle across the table. It glints in the light, and Nic glimpses the slight, oil-slick shades of magic clinging to it. "Instructions are in the pamphlet."

Nic darts a glance at Art, who looks like he's holding back from rolling his eyes. "I've used plenty of sending stones, but thanks. What then?"

Lantlit stands, spreading his hands wide with an exasperated air. "Keep it there until they arrive."

He pushes in his chair, and Nic shoots Art a panicked glance as their benefactor makes to leave.

"That's it?" Nic blurts out. "I mean, that's all?"

Lantlit turns back and smiles tightly, the gesture devoid of warmth. "That's it. Your service is appreciated, but if we haven't heard from you in a fortnight, I'll assume the worst."

And then he leaves, taking the chill with him. Nic sinks into an empty chairs, and Art leans on the back of another.

The three adventurers exchange glances, and then the girl lets out a snort.

"He was a piece of work," she says, sticking out a hand. "Also? Fuck his Miss Abernathy shit. I'm Lora. You're Nic, and…?"

"Art," Art fills in cheerily. "Guess it's a party, then."

Party. The word clanks around in Nic's chest, and he doesn't catch that he's begun to frown until Lora looks over at him, cocking her head to one side.

"Are you okay?" she asks.

Nic scrubs his expression clean immediately. "Yeah, of course. Just not too keen on dying in those woods."

"We won't," Art says firmly, though Lora's eyes remain on Nic. "With three of us? This'll be the easiest job I've ever done."

—⸺ ⌐ ◆ � ⟂ ✳ ⟂ ᪣ ◆ ⌐ ⸺—

It doesn't take long to pack up their stuff. Nic never unpacked, Art has a duffel he calls his "job bag" ready and waiting, and, well, Lora doesn't seem to *have* stuff.

She has enthusiasm. And she has a never-ending stream of idle chatter about growing up in woods that—

according to her—are nothing like the ones they're walking through now. But after an hour together, Nic starts to feel like he and Art are the ones getting the short end of the stick in this partnership.

Nic feels immediately bad for thinking it, of course. After all, what does he himself bring to the party?

Nic is halfway through a list of his qualifications when the shame seizes him, creeping towards loathing in his throat. The train of thought feels prideful and unkind, even if he would never say any of it aloud.

He swallows. Lora has as much right to be here as Art does—as Nic himself does. But something about her pokes at him in uncomfortable places he doesn't have names for, and if he can't wrangle his wayward thoughts…

Well, Nic thinks, one fist tightening around the strap of his traveling bag as Lora launches into another story about Uncle so-and-so and Cousin this-or-that, *it might be a very long trip.*

CHAPTER 4

The thing about coming of age is that you only get one chance at it.

Lora wakes up on her twenty-first birthday with a pit of excitement in her stomach so large that an hour before the dusk time ceremony, she's still scarfing the ends of her breakfast sandwich down around it.

Normally it doesn't take her a whole day to demolish two slices of sourdough, even with honey, turkey, lettuce, and butter in between them. She doesn't know why today is different. She's only been waiting for it for her entire life.

Half an hour before the ceremony, her mother is swapping her boots for heels—she always likes to be the tallest at family events; Lora inherited none of her height—and Lora is staring at the clothes strewn all around her bedroom while her brother braids her hair and she chews a notch in her lip trying to decide what to wear.

"No one gives a shit," Madison tells her. "I guarantee they'll notice more if you don't turn up before the sun starts going down."

Do you promise? *Lora wants to beg him.* Do you promise, do you promise, do you promise?

Madison goes downstairs, probably to kiss his partner and wrap their daughter in her sling, and then the whole family will walk to the clearing and Lora will walk onto the platform in—her fingers comb blindly through flannel and linen and lace—a grey shirt with cut-out flowers on the shoulders, and hand-me-down work pants that cuff at her knees.

She doesn't remember the stairs, or the path, or the walk. She only vaguely remembers the clearing, transformed as it is by the loving wreaths and boughs of yew and thyme, olives and vervain. Only the sandwich, as her father chides her that she shouldn't be hungry for the transformation, and Lora wants to tell him she's been hungry for nothing but change for years before chewing through the crusts to make him happy anyways.

She stands on the stage, and the words wash over her, and the sun goes down, and she shivers in the cooling dark and waits for it to happen, for the magic with its breath like little ants to crawl across her skin and—oh gods, oh lady moon—she can feel it, like the breeze, like a fever, like the rattle of papery seeds as the wind dislodges them, like the swell of water in your mouth before you puke—

The wind tears through her and around her and everything recedes into stillness and quiet and Lora looks down at her hands—her human hands—and cannot feel anything, not even the panic that is surely beating at the door to be let in to her numb and hollow chest.

Her eyes skate over the crowd, and her niece is bubbling and gurgling with laughter, and her brother throws back his head and howls, and her sister-in-law has blood dripping from the crevices between her teeth.

And the crickets roar like the ocean, and her vision swims in lights as fireflies patter on her head and neck and arms like rain as they fall dead from the sky in the middle of their flights.

Lora wakes up crying, and she does not meet Nic's eyes as she relieves him of his watch.

———-◆-◆-→◇◆-→◇◆--—

When Nic was eight, he got kicked in the wing by a horse.

It was his own fault. Too close to the hooves; too far from the adults.

Now, at twenty-one, he doesn't remember the day, or the horse, or what he did to provoke it, or the doctor, or the healing process. Only the blinding clarity, the screaming in his bones as he beat his wings reflexively to steady himself, and the sky refused to hold him as it always had.

It feels a little like that when magic surges through the wizard's chamber and tears a gash, easily two feet long, through Nic's chest.

He is vaguely aware of falling to his knees, vaguely aware that there should be more blood, but when he looks down, there is no blood to bleed. His skin is grey; ash tumbles from his fingertips. All the life and color has been leeched away from him.

Nic shouldn't be surprised. He's been a ghost of a man for weeks now, ever since he woke up in their wooded camp with his desperate lover leaning over him and felt nothing in his chest but howling wind. The curse has spread, draining more than just the land.

He doesn't have time for the blade or the prophecy. He doesn't have time for Art's help or their quest or anything but riding as fast as his horse will carry him in the direction of the tower.

He spends a day climbing the magical stairs.

He lasts a minute in the fight.

The wizard bends to cross the infinite span between them, faceless and nameless and shrouded in purple and black and plague, and places an indifferent hand on either side of Nic's head.

They squint at his face and cast him to the side.

"No," they say, and the room reverberates with their words. "You are not the one, and I am not planning to die at your hand."

Nic chokes on his last breath and crumbles into dust.

He wakes in the dark of the woods and believes, for a moment, that hell has finally come to claim his soul.

———-◆ ✦ ◆—◆ ✦ ◆—✦ ◆—◆ ✦ ◆-——

Art dreams the way he always dreams.

Blood on his hands. A kiss on his cheek.

Game over.

Restart.

He's having breakfast with Nadia. He eats too fast, chokes on an egg, and cannot stop choking.

His wrist burns with arcane fire. Two lives left.

It's a slow day at camp. He and Ilsa are playing drawing games in the mud by the river. A shout. Soldiers flood from the trees; he is stabbed through the gut. There are no survivors. It takes him fifteen minutes to die.

His forearm stings, throbs, aches. One life left.

Art begs Ilsa for aid. She works her spells, takes his resolve and turns it into power. They scale the mountain, open the door, flood the place with magic until his lungs ache and everyone who stands against them drowns.

There is one door left.

He opens it, steps into the dark, blinks once as his eyes adjust.

No one is there.

Gravity shifts; Art looks down.

Blood on his hands. Kisses on his knuckles.

Someone traces the curve of his palm with their mouth and licks a streak of red from his thumb.

Game over. Restart.

Restart.

Restart.

Somewhere in his third cycle, Art fades back into reality. The woods surround him, and Art anchors himself, grounding his present in their familiar smells and sounds.

When he opens his eyes, it is still dark. Art stares into the hanging sea of unfamiliar stars until they fade. When the last star disappears, he gets up and begins to cook.

CHAPTER 5

The next morning's breakfast is a somber affair. Art makes oatmeal, but despite sacrificing the precious dregs of his dried strawberries from last summer, Nic chews and swallows methodically while Lora just stares into her bowl, chasing the slivers of red around with her spoon.

"Rough night?" Art offers in an attempt to broach the subject.

Nic shrugs. Lora shrugs.

Art frowns.

"I've got sugar, if y'all want any," he tries again, taking a different approach. "Cinnamon? Cayenne? Honey?"

Nic looks up from scraping the last spoonful of oatmeal off the sides of his bowl, expression unreadable, and Art hurries to reassure him. "I can make more—"

"I'm good."

Art looks to Lora, who is staring down at her food with a look of intense concentration on her face.

"Lora?" he ventures, and her head snaps up. Art tries again. "Is the oatmeal okay?"

Lora squints at him like he's sprouted two heads and neither is speaking a language she understands.

Art drops the issue. He flubs a breath through his lips instead, deciding to let them keep their secrets. He stands, dusts his hands on his pants, and buckles on his sword.

"I'm going to scout ahead," Art announces, as if either of his companions will care. *Un-fucking-likely, if fresh-dried strawberries couldn't even capture their attention.*

He does not say *"figure your shit out while I'm gone"* and internally applauds himself for his restraint.

Art's scouting hike is uneventful, and by the time he re-enters camp, the bowls have been emptied and cleaned, and Lora and Nic are chatting superficially. They both look up when they hear him coming.

"What's the plan, boss?" Nic asks.

A profound pang of sadness shoots through Art's

chest, and he tucks the feeling away with plans to address it later. Later is, in Art's experience, a nebulous concept, and one that he fully intends to keep a comfortable arm's length away for the rest of his life.

"Well," Art responds, keeping his tone light and his affect neutral, "We don't actually know fuck-shit about each other, and I'd love to change that before we stroll headfirst into danger."

Nic frowns. "What do you want to know?"

Art shrugs. "Strengths. Weaknesses. Allergies. Relevant experience?"

Nic is still frowning, his brows scrunched together, but Lora is nodding enthusiastically and that means he's outvoted.

Art beams. The democratic process has gotten him out of more scrapes than it's ever gotten him into, and he particularly loves the way it manifests itself in groups of threes. No politics, just a solid idea, a seconding of the motion, and *action*.

"So, what?" Nic asks, and Art ignores the petulant undercurrent to his tone. "Icebreakers? Campfire songs?"

"No," Art responds with the patience of a saint. "Obviously we keep going. We have the last known location of the most recent missing supply train, and if we run into any others, we can offer protection services. I'm just suggesting that—"

Art pauses, blinking at Lora. Her hand stays raised, as if they're in an academic lecture.

"Yeah?" he prompts. "Also, appreciate it, but don't do that. You can just talk."

Lora puts her hand back down. "Why can't we be a supply train?"

Art tips his head, considering her. "Say more."

"I mean." Lora pauses, sneezes, and continues. "Supply trains are going missing. Those are the primary victims. Instead of just canvassing the woods until we find whatever is eating them"—Art watches Nic full-body recoil at the prospect of people being eaten—"while they probably hide from us, by the way—why don't we just disguise ourselves as prey?"

"So we can get eaten?" Nic contributes flatly.

Lora shoots him a confused look. "Isn't that why we're here?"

"To get *eaten?*" Nic chokes.

Art feels like this might be a good time to intervene.

"No, Lora's right," he says. "We'll have the advantage of knowing that something's coming, and a potential mark will draw them out better than a murder of adventurers clomping through the woods. There haven't been any close encounters reported, which means it's likely they'll be overconfident, sloppy. Drawing them out makes the most sense."

"I have a horse," Nic offers, though he still looks less than enthused. "Where are we going to get enough supplies?"

"We might have to head back to town," Art hums. "But I can call in some favors."

Lora clears her throat. "Empty bags packed with straw work too. And they're less weight for your horse to carry."

"I guess," Nic grumbles, looking the tiniest bit mollified at her concern.

"So it's settled," Art says with a decisive nod. "We'll head back to town, grab some fake supplies, regroup, and try again?"

His companions return the nod with varying levels of enthusiasm, and Art grins, pleased with their teamwork and its results.

"Great," he concludes. "We're only an hour or two from the edge of the woods proper, and a couple more from town. We can get everything ready, sleep at my place for the night, and then set out again tomorrow morning. Just a minor setback."

The three of them grab their things, kill the fire, and turn back the way they've come. Despite Art's earlier remarks about bonding, there's no chatting this time, each of them lost in their own thoughts.

Two hours pass, and when they haven't reached the

edge of the woods by noon, Art passes out snacks, hoping no one sees the furrow in his brow.

They keep walking.

By mid-afternoon, he's properly worried.

It's not until dusk, when the shadows stretch long around them and the sun's descent kisses the air around them with a gold-tinged chill, that Art breaks the pensive silence.

"Well," he says at last, running a hand through his hair and eyeing the periwinkle-hued trees around them. "I guess we've found what's stopping travelers from getting home."

CHAPTER 6

They make camp for the night, and no one talks.

Art digs in his bag for biscuits and passes them around with butter. Nic eats his in four bites, walks six steps away, and lays down for the night. Lora motions for the salt, and Art passes it without a word.

When Art finally speaks, it's an offer to take first watch. Lora cocks her head so far to one side that he's surprised not to hear any vertebrae crack.

"I'll do it," she says instead, so Art shrugs and heads to bed.

Art dreams of home.

Specifically, he dreams of the river.

It's less of a river and more of a stream, but it marks the western edge of his sleepy childhood town, and when he was little and learning to swim, the difference in terminology felt negligible.

Most of the parents in town have strictly forbidden their children from crossing its clear boundary under penalty of...?

It's a vague threat. Chores, probably. Mauling by wild animals, equally likely.

Damien's parents don't give a shit, and Art's give too many, so most of their adventures end with the boys collapsed on the mossy ground at the river's edge.

Today is the same. Damien lies next to Art, just far enough away to be decent, and something twists in Art's gut. This could be any afternoon, but with his luck it won't be.

He shouldn't be here. If he can't change anything, why should he relive it?

They're 16, maybe 18, and something feels wrong in Art's head, like his body is too big and too small at the same time.

Damien is asking him something, but the words are muffled through the years. Art strains, pulls against the sloth and mire submerging his bones, reaches, and catches hold of Damien's hand.

"Art?" Damien asks.

This is new, and Art panics as shocking clarity settles on the scene. He can hear the birds. He can feel the cool air drifting off the water. Damien's hand is warm and solid under his, and sunlight dances through the leaves overhead, marking dappled patters of light and shadow against his lilac skin.

"Is this real?" Art asks, voice shaking. He used to know. It's been a long time since he's known, and longer since he's wanted to. "Are you real?"

"What do you think?" Damien's black eyes turn serious, and Art takes a second to drink in his face. Pointed ears, gold freckles, hair pulled into several space-bun puffs, shy stubble peppered across his chin.

"I think..." Art moans, and the sound comes from his gut. "I think that would be too easy. I think it would be too good."

Damien's face falls, and muscle memory drives Art's other hand to cradle his boyfriend's cheek. Damien catches his hand before Art can fully bridge the gap between them.

"Better not," the other boy says, the words bitter and gentle and angry and sad, all at once. "Now needs you."

"Now sucks," Art whispers as the river laps at his feet. "I need—"

The word sticks in his throat, and Damien grins without joy, revealing a mouth full of teeth that have been replaced with jagged slivers of arkade coins.

"You don't need me," Damien says, and the water pools around Art's knees. "You want me. And it's far too fucking late for that."

Something in the water grabs hold of Art's legs, and he twists to see blood pooling in the stream as it continues to rise. Something sharp hits Art's head, and when Art looks back, Damien is holding shards of coins and teeth between his fingers and flicking them with deadly accuracy at his mark.

"We used to do this," he says. "Remember? On nights when neither of us could sleep, we'd meet behind the Arkade. We'd draw shapes on the street, and try to hit the centers."

"Damien," Art whispers as the water creeps its unwelcome touch under his shirt.

"I'd kiss you when you won, and you'd kiss me when I lost," Damien continues as if Art hasn't spoken at all. "That was before everything changed, of course. Before you changed, I should say."

"I'm sorry," Art chokes, muddy water filling up his throat.

Damien pauses. A jagged slice of gold rests on his thumb, and Art knows without being told that the next shot will be coming for his eye.

"Thanks," the other boy chirps, and Art flinches away

as the shot fires, the river drags him under, and everything goes dark.

He wakes into the woods again, his clothing sweat-soaked like a resurrection, with Damien's last words ringing in his ears.

"It's just, damn. I wish that were worth shit."

Judging from the moon, Art has only slept for half as long as he intended. His throat is still swollen with unsaid words, but with Damien gone, he swallows them down.

Later, Art promises himself. *Later, later, later.*

Art wriggles into a dry shirt, and rolls onto his other shoulder, reaching for and wrapping himself in his coat to try and drive away the chill. Sometimes he can fall back asleep after nightmares, but tonight seems determined to trap Art in its dreadful, hazy, nether drowse.

His thoughts swallow him, and the darkness swallows them, and shades and specters whirl across his vision in a tangle of ends he cannot hope to separate in this state.

Art dreams of the mundane, of a present devoid of sense. He rolls over again, twists his neck to look for Lora, sees a herding dog keeping watch over them instead. Darkness takes him under, and five minutes later Art wakes to the beginnings of another cold sweat.

He sits up and scans the camp for Lora. She's sitting where she's been all night and gives him a curious look as he rubs at his eyes.

Art points at the sky and then at her, then pantomimes resting his head on folded hands. Lora blinks at him a couple of times and shrugs.

That could mean anything, and as the whole idea was *not* to yell across their sleeping companion's body, Art stands, rifles through his pack for something to snack on, and crosses the campsite.

Lora scoots over on the fallen log she's perched herself upon, but Art settles himself easily on the grassy ground.

"I can take over if you want some extra sleep," Art offers, tearing open the paper wrappings of his homemade granola and popping a handful of it in his mouth.

Lora hesitates, staring off into the trees. "I'm not sure I want to sleep more than absolutely necessary right now."

Art makes a sympathetic noise. "Nightmares?"

Lora's eyes snap to him in surprise. "You too?"

"Oh, yeah." Art laughs, the sound startled out of him. "Every night."

Lora's brows knit together, and Art feels a stab of guilt for reacting so casually. He'd forgotten that nightmares were omens worth noting for most people. He'd forgotten that he wasn't normal.

"I haven't had them since I was a kid," Lora admits.

"Mmm." Art stuffs another handful of granola in his mouth before he can say something stupid or overshare. "Do you want to talk about them?"

Lora shakes her head. "Nothing bad even happened. It was just stupid shit."

Art sighs. "Those can be the worst kind."

Lora props her elbows on her knees, studying the ground. "I get panicky when I think about it, like something in my chest is trying to break out. I'm scared that if I go to sleep tonight, I'll have more. I feel like something's trying to *get* me."

Art nods sympathetically. "Well, if it makes you feel any better, I've been having chronic nightmares since I was..." He pauses, counting backwards on his fingers. "Sixteen? I know the feeling you're talking about, and it sucks. But dreams are just dreams, and nothing's come for me yet."

Lora huffs out a breath, and something about her expression calls Art's half-asleep vision to his mind.

"Oh," he starts, sitting up straighter. "This is a strange question, I know, but was there a dog hanging around here earlier?"

Lora freezes. "Did you... see a dog? Earlier?"

Art shrugs. "I don't know. You were keeping watch. That's why I'm asking you."

"Oh." Lora looks like she's stalling as she steadily avoids making eye contact. "Yeah. He might be… mine."

Art raises his eyebrows. "Do you have a dog?"

"Kind of?" Lora groans. "He's not *my* dog. Just *a* dog. He's been following me."

Art nods slowly.

"I can't get rid of him," Lora continues, her eyes darting quickly to his face before seeking refuge in the trees again. "Trust me. I've tried."

Art doesn't think he wants to know any more about that.

"I mean," he offers, "If he just needs a place to live so he stops stalking you, I've got room in my apartment. I get along well enough with most animals. When you get back, I can try and help you out."

Lora draws in a deep breath.

"Thank you," she says politely. "But I don't think that will fix my problem."

"The offer stands." Art shrugs. "Anyway, you should probably go to sleep. I've got things handled here."

"Thanks," Lora murmurs, accepting the chance to escape.

Art chews and swallows another handful of granola, surveying the woods he'll be watching for the next four hours.

"Actually," he muses, "I bet I know somebody who could talk to your dog. They've got to have a *speak with animals* spell or something equally useful in their collection. D'you think that would work?"

Silence is the only response, and when he looks back over his shoulder towards camp, Lora is curled up on her jacket, pretending her best to be asleep.

CHAPTER 7

Through the mire of sleep, Nic hears someone calling his name and fights his way upward like a drowning man.

He breaks through into consciousness with a scream ringing in his ears and tumbles out of bed, tripping over his own feet in his haste. The door stands slightly ajar, and Nic slams through it with one shoulder.

In the hallway, his sister Arleth stands alone, raspberry blood staining her fingers. He stares at her, and her face splits into a grin, revealing seeds between her teeth.

She's laughing at him, his sleep-fogged brain registers, but he doesn't understand why.

Until the bookcase screams.

Nic jumps, spins around, and rushes to the shelves. His asshole sister doubles over with laughter.

"Ohhh, Tumes!" she howls, invoking the god of their parents. "You thought someone was dead for real!"

Nic glowers at the bookcase, pulling books haphazardly from shelves until he finds the object of his ire—a ball of goo and glass pulsing lightly with magic, his sister's name tooled into the thin leather band around it.

"It's a dragon drill!" she chirps, appearing at his elbow. "I made it so you can practice, since you're supposed to save the world, and you can't do that if you sleep through the fucking disaster. D'you like it?"

Nic does not like it. Nic burns with fury and fear and fatigue and targetless adrenaline.

Nic would also rather swallow his sister's arts and crafts sorcery project than try to explain the raw bundle of nerves buzzing in his chest, especially to this eight-year-old thorn in his side.

"Language," he bites out instead, and Ari rolls her eyes.

"Nobody's here who cares," she retorts. "Mom and dad are at worship."

Nic's eyes narrow. "Why aren't you at worship?"

"Because I'm sick," Ari informs him, fluttering her eyelashes innocently. "And you're watching me, which is why you're not at worship, so you're welcome."

"I like worship," Nic grumbles. He doesn't know if he likes worship, but he knows he's supposed to, and that distinction hasn't done much for him in the past except drag out arguments.

Besides, he's thirteen, freshly reborn into teenagerhood. Nic doesn't like anything because teenagers don't like anything, and taking medicine with ice cream is for babies like his sister.

"You still shouldn't swear," he grumbles. "You'll get in the habit, and Mom will lose her shit."

"If I swear in front of Mom, it's because Hell itself has possessed me," his sister grumbles before letting out a gasp and draping herself dramatically against the doorframe. "Maybe that's how swearing works! Maybe there're devils of swearing who can possess people in moments of weak and infirm spirit. Maybe that's why Tumelnin forgives us when we ask because our actions aren't actually born of our own vileness. D'you think that's how it works?"

Nic grabs the device from the shelf and storms back into his room, slamming the door and twisting sharply until the old knob sticks. His sister rattles it from the other side.

"You're welcome for that too!" she shouts through the door, which is thin enough to render yelling both completely unnecessary and purposefully annoying. "The dragon drill! Seriously— how are you supposed to

save everybody from the Son of Fire if you're damn sleeping?"

"Can't hear you," Nic calls back, stuffing the contraption under a mountain of clothes to slowly suffocate. "The door's stuck!"

Ari yells something back, but Nic ignores her, already climbing up, over, and out through the window.

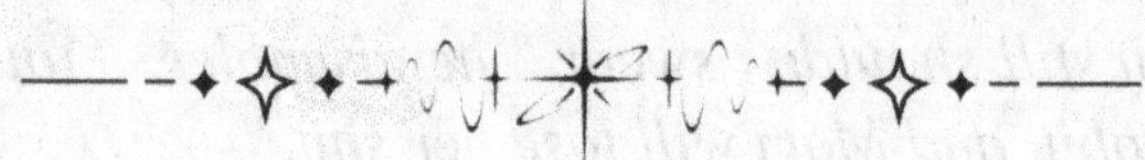

When Lora closes her eyes, she is back in the woods—her woods—in the ceremonial clearing where everything went wrong.

She can see silver and white mist between and behind the trees, and the light shines from all the wrong places, casting shadows towards her from every direction. It's empty, and the celebratory boughs look worse for wear, some dry and drained of life, some dripping ooze and crawling with flies.

There's a smell of rot hanging heavy on the air, and Lora knows instinctively that something has been left unattended for far too long.

Slowly, she circles the clearing, trailing her fingers along the top of the short stone wall which marks the border of their hallowed space. None of her family members are here, but if she strains her ears, maybe she can hear them?

Lora tries and is met with only an empty ringing in her skull.

"Don't overtax yourself," a voice rumbles behind her, and Lora whirls to see two shapes emerge from the trees, shifting into focus as though someone is in the process of correcting a child's telescope lens. "This moment is yours alone."

Lora takes a step back, staring at the creatures. They're both wolves, but like none she's ever seen before.

For one thing, they're both massive. The tips of their ears are level with the top of her head, and each paw is equal in size to one of her shoulders.

Their similarities to each other end there.

One wolf, to put things bluntly, is a horror. Its fur is ungroomed and unloved, full of mats and leaves. Its natural color is a mottled mix, painted with every shade of red and grey and brown. The effect is the same as if a regular wolf had run for miles, bathed in mud, and afterwards brought down a violent kill.

The other wolf is the picture of perfection, a soft white, with fur so clean that Lora wouldn't dream of touching it for fear of leaving behind her filthy human fingerprints.

"Stare as you like," the white wolf hums, and the other shudders with laughter, unsheathing its claws and

stretching lazily against a tree to leave deep gouges in the wood.

"Why are you here?" Lora croaks.

"To help," the white wolf says.

The terrible wolf yawns. "To correct a wrong."

"I'm sorry." Lora takes one step back and then another, until the backs of her knees bump up against a bench, and she sinks down onto it. "I don't know what I did wrong. I didn't mean to fuck it up."

"You did nothing wrong," both wolves growl, fierce enough that Lora flinches.

In a flash, both wolves have crossed the threshold of the clearing, and the light behind the trees goes out, leaving the clearing bathed by nothing but the stars. Lora lets out a cry, reaches her hands out to steady herself, and finds a wolf beneath each palm.

The white wolf glows faintly blue beneath the darkened sky, her fur warm and soft and everything Lora expected it to be. She holds still and perfect under Lora's touch.

The terrible wolf rumbles as Lora's fingers tangle in its fur. Up close she can feel that there are patches missing, hungry holes under the skin, and gaps between its ribs where dark void spills out like cold steam.

Lora draws both hands back. Everything feels wrong. She is too small, too unworthy.

"We're scaring her," the terrible wolf says harshly to its companion and folds up its limbs, settling into a heap on the ground. "I told you we would."

"She is always afraid," the white wolf snaps back. "We agreed to give her a choice, and that means we both deserve a chance to state our case."

"Speak, then," the terrible wolf says, resting its head on its paws. "I yield the first chance to you."

It looks into Lora's eyes, and she finds herself floating in the depths of its gold ringed pupils. "My offer speaks for itself."

"Fine," the white wolf says, and in a blink, she has shifted, borrowing a familiar skin that that Lora has seen in puddles and shop window reflections. Dog.

The white wolf turns her head to the terrible one, and Lora recoils at the wrongness of hearing such an ethereal, otherworldly voice come from Dog's shape. "Privately, if we may?"

The terrible wolf snorts, stands, and drags its rotten tongue across the back of Lora's hand.

"I will see you again," it promises, and then the night swallows it up.

The white wolf's version of Dog curls up at Lora's feet, fixing her with intelligent eyes, and Lora squirms. When the wolf speaks, the sound fills every corner of Lora's mind.

My gift will hold you, she intones. *It will guard you. It will give none reason to find fault. You will be soft, and loved, and cared for, all the days of your life.*

Lora's stomach twists, and she says nothing, only swallows back a hundred shames.

The Dog-wolf climbs into her lap and nuzzles her face, and Lora holds still, her every muscle bracing for the dream to change into a nightmare.

Instead, she wakes to rustling leaves, frying eggs, and the beginning of another day.

After leaving Ari and the house behind, Nic ends up where he usually does—the stables.

His parents are still busy at worship, along with most of the adults in town, which means he's free as a bird until lunch. If he's lucky, they won't return for an hour or so beyond that, busy gossiping among their fellow congregants.

As always, his favorite horse is in its stall, a gelding named Comet who was born the same week Nic was. Nic rests his forehead on the horse's neck and feels a hot exhale against his collarbone.

"I know," Nic mumbles. "I come as often as they let me."

Comet snorts and twists his neck around to pull a mouthful of food from his bag. Nic sinks to the ground with his back against the door of the stall and tries to ease the tension from his shoulders.

[NICODEMUS.]

Just like that, the tension returns. Nic sits ramrod straight, looking around wildly. There's no one here except Comet, who has paused mid-bite and fixed Nic in an unblinking stare.

This is new. This isn't part of the history Nic remembers, and he stares back, watching grass fall from the horse's mouth as it unhinges.

"I HAVE BEEN LOOKING FOR YOU," *the horse says, and Nic's bones begin to shake.*

"DO NOT RUN."

Comet tosses his head and screams, and hot wind tears at Nic's face as he cowers behind one wing. Comet stomps and kicks, and the wind catches the dust of the stall, finding its way into Nic's eyes and nose and mouth. Nic coughs and sneezes and draws in lungfuls of sand and squeezes his eyes shut, bracing for death.

Instead, the gusts roar to a climax and then subside. Nic finds himself back in the woods and, if the chills rattling his frame are to be believed, running a fever.

CHAPTER 8

Morning finds Nic in a foul mood without even the energy to feel more than vaguely bad about it. The camp is claustrophobic, the trees watch his every move, and his companions stretch his last nerve so thin that all he can feel is an all-consuming boiling under his skin. He jumps at every noise, snaps at Art when he asks about it, and nearly gets into an all-out brawl with Lora when she tells him to stop acting like a child.

A child. A *fucking child?*

Nic fumes. Even when he was a child, he wasn't allowed to act like one. He tries to come up with a cutting retort, but his head is throbbing, and the only thing he can come up with is calling Lora an "actual child."

It has the desired effect. Lora actually bares her teeth at him, making Nic laugh, and Art snaps that if they're going to waste time with a pissing contest, they can do it somewhere else.

"There isn't anywhere else," Nic growls, throwing a rock at the closest tree, hard enough to chip the bark.

He has another in hand, ready to throw, but the shadow of Art falls over him, and the other boy confiscates the rock, grabs him by the shoulders, and points him deeper into the forest.

"Somewhere to shelter if it starts raining," he orders, and Nic casts a glance at the sky.

It's grey and cloudy, which explains the migraine, which explains the irritability, which makes Nic feel guilty and then angry, with all of it balancing out into the helplessness of *trapped, trapped, trapped.*

Nic's never handled helplessness very well.

Lora snorts, sounding somewhere between derisive and approving as Nic storms off in the direction Art pointed him.

"You too." Art spins towards her, the steel in his voice leaving no room for arguments. "And three edible plants, if you can find them."

And so—both wishing they were anywhere else *with* anyone else—Lora and Nic find themselves stomping alone through the dreary, chilly, grey woods.

It's not long before Nic's stomping slows to a calmer cadence. Because his feet hurt, and it's not safe to leave heavy footprints in their wake, nothing more. Likewise, Lora—who started their quest with tightly crossed arms and a scowl that could fell trees—eventually lets the tension in her body fade.

"Sorry," she grunts at last.

The disyllable still harbors the sharp edges of resentment, and Lora sounds like someone following through with a loathsome duty, but Nic sees the olive branch for what it is.

"S'fine," he returns, forcing his white-knuckle grip on anger to relax. "Not entirely your fault, it it?"

"Nightmares have been getting to both of us, I guess," Lora mumbles, and Nic has to stop himself from visibly startling.

"How did you—? "

Lora casts a reproachful look his way. "We're all having them, stupid. The woods are fucking with all of us. Even Art. I just think he's been in other woods like this before, so he knows how to handle it better."

Shame washes over Nic, but because Lora hasn't earned the privilege of seeing him cry, he holds it back. "What are yours about?"

"Family." Lora looks away. "Yours?"

Nic chokes on a laugh. "Destiny."

They walk in silence for a bit, and then Lora motions for Nic to pause. He waits as she investigates a tall plant, examining its small flowers, buds, and leaves, then takes out a small knife and trims a bit from it.

"Try this," she says, handing it up, and Nic nibbles tentatively on the gift.

"Oh—ugh." Nic spits, grimacing. Lora is grinning when he looks over, and Nic rolls his eyes. "Sure, funny. What is it?"

"Vervain. Good for headaches," Lora answers. "Tastes like shit, but it might help."

Nic stares, and the words come out more incredulous than annoyed. "How the fuck did you know that I have a headache?"

Lora blinks. "You… smell like one?"

Nic decides he can't have heard that right, but Lora's still talking, and he can't figure out a way to ask that doesn't make him sound stupid either.

"You're all scowl-y, too," she goes on, gesturing to her forehead. "And it's grey. My brother gets migraines and pain all over when it's going to rain. He pushes through a lot, but he has to stay in bed about half the time because of them. It sucks."

"Oh." It's all Nic can think to say, and he tears off another piece of the plant, chewing reluctantly. "Thanks."

Lora shrugs, and they keep walking.

"Why are you out here?" Nic asks at last, breaking the

quiet with the question that's been rotting in the corner of his mind for days.

Lora looks up at him, startled. "With you?"

"With us," Nic clarifies. "Why'd you take this job?"

Lora shrugs. "Why did you?"

It's a brush off, but Art already knows, and if Nic is going to be trapped in these cursed-ass woods with this strange, reticent girl, it would be nice not to want to strangle her the whole time. He can barter one piece of personal information from his closely guarded store.

"I need Art to help me find something," he admits, ignoring the flash of surprise on Lora's face. "He was planning to take this job with or without me, so I figured it was a good enough way to pass the time."

Lora nods slowly, and Nic can see her tucking the information away.

"Your turn," he prompts after another minute passes.

Lora sighs.

"I just wanted to *do* something," she says at last, and the yearning in her voice hits Nic like a sledgehammer. "Something normal. Something worthwhile. My brothers, my cousins, my parents—they've all been on quests. Hell, most of them regularly go on quests. Madison's only staying close to home to help his partner with the baby, and… I can do it. I know I can."

She looks at Nic with eyes that pierce right through him. "I was really sick, for a while. I'm still sick, I guess, since it's the kind of thing that never really goes away. There's ticks all over the woods I grew up in, so you have to be careful. And sometimes, even when you're perfectly careful, you miss one. So I got bit when I was eight or something, and then I got better, and then I got sick again. And it just kept getting worse. I'm lucky my dad studied medicine and keeps up with things, but even with all his work, I've only gotten this much of my health back in the last year."

Lora swallows hard, and Nic finds that his own throat is tight.

His companion recovers, continuing, "And nobody treats me like I'm slowing them down, but I know that I am. Whenever they need to be fast or be careful, they don't ask me to come. I'm probably more careful than all of them because I live with my limits every day, but they don't *know* that because they only notice when I miss my baseline. But, like, my body was the first person in my life to consistently let me down. I'm the one who's missing out on my own life, and I still have to be on speaking terms with her if we're ever going to get anything done. So I've gotten good at negotiating. I've gotten better at not asking too much of us. I protect us, but they all act like *they* have to protect *me*, just because sometimes I have flare-ups, and sometimes I'm tired, and sometimes they watch me get frustrated and cry about things they don't understand. I had to *beg them* to—"

Lora stops, scrubs at her face, starts again. "I have to beg them to let me do *normal fucking things*, and even when they say yes, things are still different. And I'm tired of being different. And I'm tired of fending off the belief that *different* means *worse*, and I'm tired of watching them be proud when I succeed but prepared when I fail. I just wanted to surprise them instead of fulfilling their lowered expectations. Like, 'Oh yeah, that's our Lora! We're *soooo* proud of her for eating breakfast and spending a couple hours in the garden without needing a nap afterwards!'"

Lora looks away, gritting her teeth. "I just had to get away. Do something new, something they'd be proud of. I wanted to see what I could do without anyone having expectations. I'm tired of listening to people give me doom-and-gloom reminders of everything that could possibly go wrong before I've even started anything."

Nic nods along as she finishes, pretending the lump in his throat is from the lingering bitterness of the herb and nothing else.

"Sorry," Lora adds sheepishly. "You said, like, one sentence and I responded with the last 12 years of my life story."

Nic keeps his eyes on the path, choosing his words carefully. "It makes sense. I'm sorry. It's hard to know that people are looking at you and seeing something else superimposed on top. Whether they see a better version or a worse version, it hurts to be telling them who you are and still watch them be surprised when you're right."

"Yeah," Lora says quietly, looking at him out of the corner of her eye. "You get it."

"Yeah," Nic replies. "I think I do."

He's drawing in a breath to say more, potentially even to part with another trinket of personal information from his hoard, when Lora stops walking.

"Do you smell that?" she asks, nose scrunching up in disgust.

"What?" Nic jokes, "Someone else with a migraine?"

Lora shakes her head and darts off the path and into the bushes. Nic sighs, does a quick scan of their surroundings, then pulls his wings close to his back and follows her.

It doesn't take long for Nic's nose to catch up, especially once the ground starts making upsetting sounds beneath his feet. Dry, brittle grass crackles and crunches with every step, even as putrid pockets of moss squelch and smear under his boots.

"Lora?" he calls, picking his way through the impossible sludge. "I don't think we're going to find anything edible here."

He catches sight of her then, kneeling on a rock, bent double as she levers a stick through the soil with frantic motions.

"Lora?" Nic tries again.

"Something's wrong," Lora answers, forcing a small, round stone from the dirt. The smell triples, and Nic gags, pulling his shirt up to cover his nose.

"Maybe we should leave it alone," he suggests.

Lora shakes her head, still consumed by her task.

"Something's wrong," she says again. "Help me dig?"

Nic sighs, reluctantly lowering himself into a squat and sinking his hands into the forest floor. He has to stop himself from gagging again as his fingers make contact with the ooze of conflicting textures. The dirt beneath the ground is olive-colored and dry like coarse rice flour. Nic has had his hands in a fair amount of soil, but never anything as deeply *wrong* as this.

The roots snaking through the earth are stiff and calcified, off-white like slivers of bone, and Nic's stomach turns as they snap against his touch. The only thing he's seen that's even come close to this level of lifelessness is the blighted crops on Beau's family land, and even that soil-turned-ash didn't reek of corruption the way this place does.

Nic feels the same frenzy that has overtaken Lora creeping into his body as well. There's something *here*, something *wrong* under the ground, and he's not sure he'll be able to leave until they've pulled it up and burned it alive.

So lost is he in his disgust that Nic doesn't notice the ripples traveling through the ground behind him, the creak and groan of old branches swaying, as thicker, thornier roots rise from the ground like fingers and close their grasp around his ankle.

Nic lets out a yell, all concerns about the evil in the ground drowned out by his instinct to survive, and Lora full-body startles, broken from her trance as well.

"What?" she yelps, but Nic can only manage panicked grunts, twisting and writhing and gesturing towards his battle with the roots wrestling for control of his legs.

"Oh! Fuck! Oh, shit!" Lora shouts, scrambling to his side.

"Get them *off!*" Nic pants, claustrophobia gripping his throat and lungs. "Fuck!"

"I'm trying!" Lora whimpers.

She pulls out a knife, sawing at the roots, but Nic yells again as the thorns sink deeper into his boot, piercing their way through the leather.

The roots have snaked further up his legs, and Nic watches in horror as the ground crumbles away from the spot where they emerged, collapsing in on itself as the roots constrict, dragging him towards the earthy maw.

"Please," Nic begs again, but Lora is cursing, scooting back as new roots crawl from the soil, slithering around her wrists.

She looks up, meeting Nic's panicked gaze with eyes like saucers, and then, in the space of time it takes Nic to blink, Lora is gone, replaced with a dog.

Nic blinks again. The image remains. The roots, equally confused, can't tighten fast enough to adjust for their prey's change in size, and the dog rears back, snarling and shaking them off.

Still struggling to keep up, Nic has barely processed that Lora is *a dog now* before he is abruptly forced to reckon with a new problem.

Lora-as-a-dog barks twice and then rockets past him, disappearing into the woods.

Fuck, Nic thinks, collapsing onto his back on the ground and choking out a sobbing laugh as the roots pull him closer to an early grave. He's going to die in these woods, and no one will tell Beau, and no one will tell Ari, because the only person who knows he's here would rather save her own ass than stick around to help save his.

But, after all, he should be used to being on his own.

Nic grits his teeth and rolls onto his stomach, straining to airlift himself out before the roots can tangle themselves into his wings, too.

So much for bonding, he thinks bitterly, and

immediately regrets it as Lora—as the dog—as the Lora-dog—barrels back into the clearing with Art in tow.

"Help!" Nic hollers, and the boy drops to the ground, digging in his bag.

Behind Art's back, Lora has tumbled from a dog into a girl again, scaling the nearest tree and leaning down to catch hold of Nic's arm. Nic grasps her intent immediately and nearly weeps with relief, redoubling the beating efforts of his wings and hoping desperately as Art pulls out an ax and hefts it with determination that the other boy intends to chop through the roots at their source and not through Nic's leg.

There's a splintering *crack* of ax meeting root, and Nic cries out gratefully, lurching forward in the air as Lora shifts her grip to his upper arms.

"I've got you!" she gasps, fingers tangled in his shirt.

More awful, meaty thumps run through the clearing, and then another crack frees one of Nic's legs entirely. His relief is thick enough to choke on, and Nic hugs that leg to his chest before kicking at the trunk of the tree until the splinters of root crumble off, pattering against the ground like spring rain.

A few more chops, and his other leg is free. Lora drags him up onto the branch, and Nic clings equally to it and her.

"I've got him!" Lora yells hoarsely down to Art, and

there is a *whooshing* noise as a wave of heat and stink sweeps over the clearing.

When Nic looks down, the grass is burning, and the roots are shriveling back into the earth, dragging tendrils of flame along with them.

"Come on!" Art shouts, stomping at the dozens of little shoots attempting to ensnare him as well.

Nic and Lora half-climb, half-fall from the tree, and the three adventurers run, leaving nothing but smoldering remains in their wake.

———-◆ ✧ ◆-→ ⁀ † ✴ † ⁀ ⁀ ◆ ✧ ◆-———

When they get back to camp, Art throws himself into dinner prep, and Lora watches as Nic roots around in the woods for the better part of an hour, finally approaching her with a mid-sized stick. Her companion stops a few steps away and holds out the offering.

Lora arches a brow.

"If this is a joke about dogs and fetch," she says flatly, "I'm not in the mood."

"I… didn't think of that." Nic has the decency to look embarrassed, at least. "It's meant to be an olive branch? I don't think the climate's right in these woods, though, so I settled for birch."

Lora crosses her arms, regarding him. "I'm listening."

"I was an ass," Nic confesses. "I projected my own fears and insecurities onto you. Whether or not we'd have come together otherwise, we're here now. The woods already seem intent on tearing us to pieces. There's no sense in helping them along."

Lora eyes him a moment more before taking the stick and turning it over a couple of times in her hands.

"Thank you," she says finally. "Apology accepted."

Surprise ripples across Nic's face. "Just like that?"

"I mean," Lora scoffs, "If you're insincere and keep being a dick, I'll take it back. But it's a nice stick, and you looked like you were swallowing rocks the whole apology, so I'm inclined to believe that's good too."

Nic nods slowly, looking like he's seeing her for the first time.

Lora hesitates. "You won't be horribly offended if I put it in the fire now, right?"

Nic laughs, and Lora grins, and the ice between them shatters at last.

Chapter 9

Nic wakes up to the comforting smell of horses, to the prickle of hay on his skin, and the familiar ache of muscles still settling into the rhythm of manual labor. He breathes deeply, an ache swelling in his chest, though he doesn't know why. Piecemeal memories flit across his mind—roots, thorns, ghosts of an adventure from which he never returned, and Nic goes to sit up.

A weight on his shoulder stops him, and then Beau yawns, resettling his head against Nic's chest.

"Nightmare?" Nic's fiancé rumbles, and Nic stares into the dim rafters of the barn.

"I don't think I get those," he answers, uncertain why the truth tastes false on his tongue. "Just dreams and stranger dreams."

Beau chuckles sleepily. "Strange dreams, then?"

Nic shakes his head, nods, shakes it again.

"Clear as mud," Beau yawns again.

His shoulders are warm atop Nic's arm, still flushed with the echoes of a sunburn, and Nic feels a pang of envy as his fiancé breathes, bare chest rising and falling in the dark.

Nic's own chest is smothered under his best makeshift binder. Beau's the only one who Nic's ever allowed to see him undressed down to it, and Nic still hasn't gotten up the confidence to let his fiancé see any more. Beau's never pushed, but Nic still feels like he's failing, failing, failing...

"Hey," Beau says softly, nudging the top of his head against Nic's chin. "Stop angsting. My parents won't think twice of me sleeping out here. I used to do it all the time. Only stopped after I realized that mattresses were invented for bitches with chronic pain."

"I don't like lying to them," Nic whispers. "It feels wrong."

"You don't have to. I'll lie to them for both of us."

It's a joke, but it makes Nic think of worship and repentance and shame and packing up his bags in the middle of the night.

Beau kisses Nic's bicep, working his way up Nic's neck until he reaches his throat, until he reaches his mouth, and Nic lets out a soft noise, wrapping his arms tighter around the love of his life. Everything is simpler in the early mornings, in the hay, in the liminal space that only the two of them are allowed to occupy.

"I thought I was going to die," Nic murmurs in between kisses.

"I won't let you," Beau vows, fingers tangling in Nic's hair.

The ache feels like it will split Nic's heart in half. "You weren't there."

Beau tugs him closer, upsetting their balance, and the boys roll until somehow Nic has come out on top. Beau smiles up at him with a fondness in his eyes that makes Nic feel like running.

Or maybe, just maybe, like staying.

"Guess you'll have to take me everywhere you go," Beau grins. "How else am I supposed to keep you alive?"

"Forever?" Nic asks, brushing scraps of straw from Beau's cheek.

"If you want," Beau answers lightly. God, Nic envies his boldness, his sureness, the way he won't let anyone damn him except himself.

A worry flickers across Beau's brow, and Nic realizes that he hasn't answered, lost in his own thoughts.

"I want," he swears, joining his lover's lips with his. "I want, I want, I want."

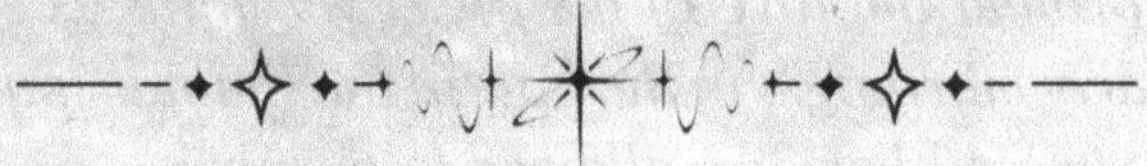

Lora's head has barely touched her pillow before a cool breath skates across her ear.

"Wake up."

She scrambles into a defensive crouch, finds herself in the Wrong Woods again. The terrible wolf pads towards her with near-silent steps.

"No time for wasting, sister," it rumbles. "The veil is thin, and you must choose tonight."

"What am I choosing?" Lora asks.

"One of us," the wolf says, and a flash of lightning cuts the clearing in two. When Lora opens her eyes again, an afterimage of the white wolf is seared in her vision, though the horrible wolf remains the only one in the clearing with her. She blinks rapidly, rubbing at her eyes to clear them.

"There is a way that things go," the terrible wolf says, stepping closer, "When humans take the forms of beasts. It works for many."

Lora looks up into its eyes but does not let herself fall all the way under the golden pools' spell this time.

"But?"

"But not for all."

Lora's heart skips a beat, a traitorous surge of hope in her chest. "I could try again? Be like the others?"

"No," the wolf says sternly. "Pay attention. You have seen the dog. You have seen me. Do I look like a forest wolf?"

The hope sinks into Lora's gut as quickly as it came.

"What are you?" she whispers.

"What are you?" the wolf echoes, stalking towards her until it is close enough that Lora has forgotten to be afraid. "What is anyone? It's not a polite question to ask."

Lora rolls her eyes without thinking, and the wolf barks with laughter.

"You are not afraid of me," it observes.

Lora looks at the grass, pulls it up by the roots and crumbles the dirt through her fingertips. "I'm tired of being afraid."

"That does not mean there are not things out there worth fearing."

"Is that all you are?" Lora retorts. "Something to fear?"

The wolf lowers its head—when did it get so close? she could touch it, if she dared—and breathes winter's chill through her hair. Lora looks up.

"There are things to fear," the wolf says. "I do not

fear them. There are things which fear. I am made of that which frightens them. You have many things to fear, but I do not intend to be one of them."

Lora shivers, and the wolf lies down, crossing one paw over the other in front of itself.

"Are you ready?" it asks.

"Ready?"

"Have you made your choice?"

Its eyes bore into her, drilling through her until Lora is full of holes. Thunder rolls across the sky, and the wind picks up, whistling through her like a child's pan flute.

"It's just..." Lora clenches her fists. "Neither of these are normal choices."

The wolf says nothing, only watches her.

Lora continues. "I don't want to get it wrong again—"

"You did not get anything wrong."

In a flash, the white wolf has joined her twin. "This is a gift, not a punishment."

Lora rubs at her head, the dull beginnings of a migraine thrumming through her skull.

"Do I have to say it?" she whispers. "I want them to be proud of me. I don't want anyone to laugh."

Dog creeps out from behind the white wolf, running to

Lora and shoving his head under her hand. He whines softly, and Lora flinches, winding muddy fingers up in his fur as a soft rain begins to fall.

"That's not fair." The terrible wolf lowers its gaze to Dog and growls. "We had an agreement. She gets to choose honestly."

"She will," the white wolf soothes, still standing at her sibling's side. "But they deserve to say goodbye."

"I don't want to be different," Lora breathes. An apology.

"You are already different," the horrible wolf breaks into a grin. "Why not become a little bit ungovernable, too?"

Lora looks at the white wolf, and her grip on Dog's fur loosens. Her hand hovers over Dog's head, removed from him in every meaningful way.

"What did you say?" she asks the wolf. "About your gift?"

"You will be beloved," the white wolf murmurs. "A pillar of comfort in a harsh and unyielding world."

Lora looks at Dog, and when she speaks, there is an old poison in her words. "You don't bring any comfort to me."

Dog whimpers, slinking backwards with his tail between his legs.

"Time is short," the monstrous wolf says solemnly. "What is your choice?"

Lora does not look at Dog, her gaze catching on the horrible wolf's chest instead, fixing on the steady red-purple glow that pulses under its fur like a star.

She sniffs, throat swollen with unsaid words. She scoops up a few, holds the inadequate clay in her hands and tries to mold it into the shape of anything but an apology. Her cheeks are wet. Is it the rain? When did she begin to cry?

"I'm sorry," Lora whispers.

"For what?" The terrible wolf asks, teeth folding into a smile.

Lora shakes her head. For what, indeed? For betraying Dog, a gift she had never wanted, bound up in the wrappings of shame and inadequacy? For crying in front of the terrible wolf, who stands here to offer her everything she's ever been afraid to want; everything she's afraid she might simply be too weak to be? For doing things wrong? For making things right?

For wanting?

Lora reaches out, fingers coming to rest over the terrible throbbing chest of the horrible, monstrous wolf. The last inch feels as far as a mile.

"I want..." she begins. It feels important to say it, as creation stills its breath to listen. "I don't want what I got

the first time. I want to try again."

The horrible wolf lets out a heavy breath, leaning in to wrap its body around Lora's as though her answer has freed it of some awful restraint.

"We will do wonders together," it purrs.

And then, before Lora can stop it, the wolf surges forward and locks its terrible jaws around Dog's throat.

Lightning explodes, thunder crashes, Dog screams, and Lora wakes with guilt in her stomach and copper on her tongue.

CHAPTER 10

Nic rouses himself sometime around midnight, drifts into the woods to pee, and returns Art's companionable nod as he crosses the threshold into camp again.

"Ready to sleep yet?" Nic asks softly, settling down on the ground beside the other boy. Art shrugs, gazing up at the sky.

"How do the stars look?" Nic prompts, after another moment has elapsed.

Art pulls a folded booklet from a side pocket of the go-bag currently resting at his feet and passes it over to Nic. "Not bad. I'd say we're flush with our original isocosm, if not still within it."

Nic pauses in an attempt to puzzle out the sentence without Art's help. He gives up once he feels the furrows in his brow starting to take root. "Say again?"

"Sorry." Art laughs and shakes his head. "I've spent too much time around speculatists. Where'd I lose you?"

"Flush with an isocosm?"

"Right."

Art takes a deep breath, and Nic watches his shoulders rise and settle again before he speaks. "So, there's this theory that the things we see before us, that which we can touch, isn't all that there is."

"Religion," Nic interrupts dryly, nodding.

"Sure, whatever." Art waves a hand dismissively. "There's overlap with religion in everything. Anyway, if you're trying to describe things you can't touch, you start getting into made-up word territory real fast. Isocosm came first, and it means *a 'container of stuff that the people who live there can touch.'* Spooky forest we can't leave? An isocosm. Everywhere you can reach by regular means, back in the place where Glenhurst is? An isocosm. Following?"

Nic shrugs. Art nods and keeps going.

"Once you've got a bunch of abstract isocosms, you have to figure out a way to start defining the differences. Somebody decided it was important to be able to talk about the idea of *whatever one we're in right now*, and that became the procosm. This is our procosm." Art gestures to the woods. "Lantlit and Gaia are in the Glenhurst isocosm, which is their procosm, but to us it's just another isocosm. When we get back, it'll be our procosm again."

Nic nods again, slower this time. He's still waiting for the part where Art starts to make sense, but he appreciates the other boy's use of the word *when* rather than *if*.

"So, an isocosm is a thing, and the procosm is *our* thing—in the present, specifically, because there's also an urcosm, but that starts to get tricky when we veer into religious folks who want to talk about the Urcosm with a capital U. Most of us just use the word on a personal level to talk about someone who theoretically traverses the veil between isocosms." Art pauses, an undercurrent of excitement thrumming through his next words, like some old creature stirring in its sleep. "Actually, I suppose that's us, now. We're in pericosm space at least. Anyways, for crosscosm travelers, whatever place they originated from would be their urcosm, with a lowercase 'u.'"

Nic scrunches up his face. Blinks. Nods.

Art seems to notice Nic's patience evaporating and cuts his explanation mercifully short.

"Anyway. The pericosm is the concept of a liminal, mostly habitable space at a cosm's border, and flush just means we're still pressed pretty tightly up against our urcosm, the one with Glenhurst and our lives."

"Flush..." Nic grabs onto the lifeline. "Like carpentry?"

Art nods enthusiastically.

"Okay," Nic says, mirroring the other boy's nodding, though significantly slower. "That's good, right? How do you know?"

Art draws in a breath.

"The abridged version," Nic hurries to add.

"Stars," Art answers simply, changing course and pointing to the sky. "They're the same as our urcosm's."

"Really?" Nic tips his head, regarding the sky. "Is it that easy to tell?"

Art hesitates. "You still want the short answer?"

"Please."

"…no. It's not that simple."

Nic flashes his companion a slight smile, and Art returns it. A breeze whistles through the woods—*through the* pro*cosm,* Nic thinks, though he's not entirely sure he's got that correct—and Art yawns, long and drawn out.

"You should go to sleep," Nic offers. "It's close enough to my watch that I don't mind starting early, and I'll grab another couple hours when Lora gets up."

Art nods idly and gazes up at the sky again, running a hand through his sandy blonde hair as the moonlight casts it in silver.

"I was in an isocosm with three moons, once," he says softly, like confessing a secret.

"Oh?" Nic says. He doesn't know what else to say.

"Thanks," Art says, picking up his go-bag with a faraway look to his eyes. "Good night."

"Good night," Nic echoes.

He watches Art walk back to his bedroll and lie down before he tears his eyes away. *Three moons…*

Nic's not sure he's ever felt quite so out of his depth.

Art dreams the way he always dreams, with a sword in his hand and three moons in the sky. He dreams of Taunneau, the place he considers his truest home,

There aren't three moons tonight, of course. Every four months, when the moon cycles align and the sky goes dark, Taunneau and all her occupants suffer under a night unlike all others. One of darkness, ghosts, and lost hopes.

Colloquially, they call it Monster Night.

So tonight, Art dreams of camp, of last suppers taken with comrades just in case this next fight is the one they lose.

His traveling party sits spread out around the fire.

Nadia, their de facto leader, with her cousin Amari. Jordan and Ishard, the twins. Banks and his husband Harrison. And Ilsa, the youngest member of the team— until Art came along, adopted into the group like a stray kitten with blood in its fur.

Ilsa moves to sit next to him now, balancing a bowl of soup between her elbows as she finishes pulling back her hair, still wet from their afternoon swim.

"Are you ready?" Art's hero asks, tying off her last braid.

She's cast some sort of magic fire on the slender antlers sprouting from her forehead, and they illuminate her face in a soft purple glow. Her lipstick is black, her eyelids are done in silver, and two sliverseeds of backup wands, ready to be summoned to full size at a moment's notice, run through the industrial piercings of her elven ears.

She looks like a dream. She looks like a nightmare.

If Art didn't have someone to get back to…

"Artham?"

She's put the soup down in her lap and thumps Art in the shoulder with her recently freed hands, breaking him from his trance.

"As ready as I'll be," he answers, taking a bolstering sip of the spiced hot chocolate that Nadia makes special every time the dark night comes around.

For courage, she says.

Art doesn't know if he believes in courage. He believes in necessity, and he believes in not dying. How he feels about the two hasn't ever been part of the picture.

Ilsa waves a hand in front of his face.

"Snap out of it," she orders. "You're with me tonight, and if you're off your game, we'll both be killed."

"I know," Art says. "Ilsa..."

Ilsa arches a brow while Art hesitates. "Out with it."

He isn't ready. He has to be ready.

"What happens if I die here?"

"What, tonight?" Ilsa frowns, catching his wrist and turning it over to eye the markings on it. "You've got two lives left, and a tyrant to kill. You'll be fine."

"No," Art says, uncharacteristically serious. "If I die all the way in a place that isn't mine, what happens to me?"

Ilsa regards him for a long moment.

"Nobody knows," she says at last. "Maybe you go home."

"Maybe," Art echoes, worry carving furrows in his brow like the river they've made camp alongside.

Ilsa watches him a moment more before letting out a sigh. "You're asking my opinion? As a sorcerer and speculatist?"

Art nods.

"I think you're just dead," Ilsa says, flat and blunt, the way Art needs. "You turn into one more ghost in a crowd, trying to take back what you've lost from those of us who still have it."

Art looks away and nods again. He doesn't know what he hoped to hear, but Ilsa's speculation doesn't fill the void in his soul the way he hoped it would.

"Hey," Ilsa says, gentler this time. "Don't worry about it. Best way to avoid death is by not dying, right?"

Art has to roll his eyes at that, and Ilsa grins.

"Sure," Art deadpans, standing and offering a hand to help her up. "If it's that simple, why doesn't everyone do it?"

The sun's last rays melt below the horizon, and Ilsa looks to the woods.

"You can ask the dead when they come," she jokes, painting a thin veneer of humor over the nerves Art knows they're both feeling. "If any of them feel like talking."

The first ten to fifteen ghosts never feel like talking. Art leaves the spectral birds, squirrels, and rabbits alone to remember what grass feels like beneath their feet and readies himself for the rest.

The faces of the dead blur together as the ghosts of every monster and person they've killed come back to exact their last revenge. Art grits his teeth, presses his back to Ilsa's, and cuts through them all.

Around the fire, the rest of his party is doing the same in groups of twos.

Put the past behind you, Art thinks, but don't let it sneak up and stab you in the back.

And then—he forgot about this part, or maybe he didn't know it was coming to begin with—Art hears a yell, spins, and locks blades with himself.

"Art?" Ilsa calls, blasting the ghost of a soldier into scraps of burning ash. "You good?"

"Fine," both Arts jump to reassure her.

Art feels his eyes widen, and his mirror grins.

"Art?" Ilsa asks again.

"It's me," Art says, blocking a swing that intends to take off his head. "A ghost of me!"

Ilsa curses, and Art feels the cold air of the night on his back as the echo of himself catches his arm and drags him away from his partner.

They're equally matched, except for the fact that Art has been fighting for his life for an hour, and Other-Art seems as fresh as the grave they didn't dig for him.

"Why is he here?" Art shouts to Ilsa as his sword is

wrenched from his grasp, leaving him grappling with his opponent bare-handed.

"You died," Ilsa shoots back.

"What?"

"Sucks, right? All the dead come back. Happens when we lose someone from our side too. You're just one of the unlucky few who's still around to see it."

Art forces a knee upwards, driving it into his opponent's stomach.

"You're right," he shouts back.

"Say more?"

"It does suck!"

Art loses track of himself in the fight, wrestling with the shade of his former self.

"Why are you doing this?" one of them manages, fresh bruises blooming around their eye.

"I'm not 'doing' shit," the other grunts, and Art is both and neither and lost.

A searing blast of purple light erupts, and Art is thrown violently back into his body as the two of them are broken apart. Another flash cuts through the air, and the Art-that-is-not-Art screams as their chest is engulfed in supernatural flames.

The rest of the ghosts have either died again or

disappeared, and Art drags himself up from the ground in the silent shell of their former camp. All he sees is Ilsa, rubbing grit and dust from her wand, and Art swallows his fear and forces himself not to look for the rest of his family among the bodies of the dead.

Not-Art lies smoldering on the starlit grass, and Art flinches as Ilsa drives a spiked heel through the ruins of his chest.

"Thank you," he manages, approaching from behind as she finishes off the echo of his past. "I'd have died again, if you weren't here."

"Of course," Art's hero replies. She turns, and Art watches the purple light cast shadows across her face. "I'm sorry, Art."

"Sorry?"

The word has barely passed his lips before bright pain blooms in his gut.

Ilsa catches him as he starts to fall, easing him to the ground as Art chokes and gasps on a mouthful of blood as it dribbles down his chin.

"I'm sorry," Ilsa says again, gently pulling the silver dagger from his side. Dawn creeps into the sky behind her, and she cradles his cheek with her palm. "You understand. I have to be sure."

Ilsa passes a hand over his eyes, and Art's senses fade to black.

He dies in the world of Taunneau and wakes to his real life.

Again.

CHAPTER 11

The first sign that something's wrong with Art is when he puts sugar instead of salt in the eggs he cooks for breakfast. Lora recoils at the first whiff of her plate, and Nic, warily, gets a forkful to the tip of his tongue before giving up.

Art eats every bite of his double-loaded plate without complaint, poring over the array of maps and charts he's spread across the ground.

Nic and Lora exchange glances, and when Nic announces that they're going to forage for something else—Lora shakes her head urgently in the background; Nic changes tactics—to *help* Art with *lunch* prep, Art barely spares them an acknowledging nod.

So, Lora and Nic find themselves, for the second time in as many days, tromping through the woods in search of something edible.

"No chasing odd smells today," Nic entreats. "Please?"

Lora laughs, letting an exaggerated shudder travel through her shoulders. "Not on my life."

Nic eyes her for a moment. "You look… different this morning."

Panic flares in Lora's gut, and she quickly quells it. *We're okay. It was just a nightmare.*

"What kind of different?" Lora asks instead.

"Lighter?" Nic muses. "I don't know, exactly."

Lora hums and cants her head to the side, testing the length and weight of her limbs in her mind. There's a static fuzz running underneath her thoughts and a strange silence from the corner of her mind where Dog usually sprawls while they're in human form, but that could mean anything.

It was a nightmare. It doesn't mean anything.

"I don't know what to tell you," Lora finally admits. "I'm just… here."

"Okay." Nic bobs his head. "Great."

They walk in silence for a few minutes, and then Nic finally starts the question Lora's been waiting to hear him ask since yesterday.

"Why didn't—"

"Why didn't I tell you both about the lycanthropy?" Lora interrupts.

She crosses her arms tightly, shoulders slipping towards the defensive hunch her cousins used to tease her for. *Like a dog guarding food.*

"Because fuck you," she continues. "It's my business."

"No," Nic hurries to assure her. "I wasn't going to ask that. It was something else, something you said yesterday. You had to beg your family to let you do normal shit. Why didn't they… surely it can't have all been because you were sick, right? Don't lycan have increased strength? Sick for you is probably peak health for someone like me."

The tension leaves Lora's shoulders in a rush, and she sighs, running a hand through her hair.

"I don't think that's how being disabled works. Or how an overprotective family works. But even if it were, it wouldn't have mattered. I wasn't lycan before a week ago."

"A week?" Nic repeats. "As in *one* week?"

"It's a coming of age thing." Lora frowns. "Tradition says that the first twenty years at minimum must be lived on two legs, before the next forty can be lived on four."

Nic's brow furrows. "Are you planning to die at 60?"

A knot of something—Rage? Jealousy? Grief?—

twists itself in Lora's chest. She tries for safety, for a joke.

"I mean, personally," she says, "I've been expecting to die any day since I was fifteen, so excuse you."

Nic coughs, once.

"Sorry." Lora flushes. "Um. It's probably just left over from when people didn't live as long. Or a joke about how if you split your adulthood evenly between forms, you get eighty years instead of forty. I don't remember what my parents said when I asked about it."

Nic asks another question, but Lora is too busy to hear it. There's something in the back of her head, pooling onto the floors of her mind like sand and making everything just a little harder than it's supposed to be, and she starts running through the mental checklist she keeps for times like this—when her interoception fails, and she has to manually deduce what's wrong with her body.

Lora trials a couple of breaths and decides that even though her breath is coming short, her throat and lungs are unobstructed. Her head is fine, aside from the fog. Her neck and shoulders are a little hot, but nothing that being under the sun can't explain.

Lora starts over, working her way up from the bottom of the list. Her legs raise no complaint, other than the usual amount of soreness in her ankles, knees, and hips. Her calves feel tight, but nothing worth panicking about.

She skips ahead again to check her heart rate. Racing for sure, but from the panic? Or its source?

She's missing something; she knows it and starts again. The top of her head, her throat, shoulders, chest—what else is there?

Oh, right, she realizes, clarity washing over her like the dawn as Well-Lora's world takes one last gasp before the tidal wave of pain converts her. *My gut.*

I'm sick. It's the usual pain.

Nic surges forward to catch Lora as she gasps and doubles over, but she shakes her head, faster and faster until he stops and pulls back.

"What's wrong?" Nic asks, low and urgent. "Lora, what's wrong?"

Lora laughs, whimpers, and chokes out a noise like a hurt animal.

"It's okay," she breathes, though the shaking hand she extends towards him says otherwise. "I'm just sick. Help—*hhhh*—Help me sit? Help me sit?"

Nic holds her hand, offers his other hand, and generally stands there feeling useless as she eases herself to the ground with little input.

Lora grunts as her knees buckle on the last couple of

inches, folding one leg under her and then the other.

"What do you need?" Nic begs, trying not to stare at her in horror. "What can I do?"

Lora waves a hand at him, one hand kneading heavy circles in her gut. "Nothing. It's okay. It'll pass. Sorry—I—"

The last of the sentence escapes in a pained exhale, all breath and no words.

"*Lora,*" Nic pleads.

Lora grits her teeth and tries to smile at him anyway. "It's normal. Just—I just—I have to ride it out. I can ride it out."

"Is this better?" Nic asks, sinking to a crouch and peering around the spilled hair shielding her face. "I thought you said you were better? Why is it happening?"

Lora gives a winded laugh and a wild shrug.

"It just happens. It's okay. A bad one, sure," she pants. "Not too bad. Worse. Worse than usual. Old bad. Not the worst."

Another spasm of pain tears through her, and Nic's hands ball into helpless fists as Lora's expression twists into a grimace.

"What can I do?" Nic asks again.

Lora rocks mournfully. Both arms are wrapped around her waist again, and she's scooted up her shirt to tuck her hands under, digging her nails into handfuls of skin.

"It's okay," she breathes, and Nic finds himself staring at her arms. Something pulses under the skin of them, like a heartbeat, only wrong in every possible way. "It might be the stress. Almost dying. That can upset things."

Nic tears his eyes away, returning back to her face. Lora's own eyes are tightly closed, and an eyelash falls onto her cheek.

Then another.

And another, raining like splinters against the pale blush of her skin.

"Maybe," Lora pants, "Maybe I'm eating wrong? Too many eggs. Not enough... normal. Normal stuff. Too many strange things?"

"Lora—"

Nic watches fur sprout from Lora's eyebrows, watches her cheekbones shift, watches the flesh of her cheek *tear*, exposing teeth and gums and void and fur— *so much fur*.

"It could be anything," Lora sobs, and the words reach Nic from far away as Lora's shivers turn into shudders and tremors that feel like they're shaking the very earth they're both kneeling on. "It's okay, though. It'll pass. I'm okay. I'll be okay. It'll pass—"

Nic stares transfixed as a monster—the angles of a dozen fighting wolves, crammed into the too-small, too-soft mold of a girl—sheds Lora like snakeskin, tips its head back, and *screams*.

—·✦·+⌢∪†⋇†∪⌢+·✦·—

Lora can tell from the way Nic is looking at her that he expected the recovery time to take much longer, but when the sick is gone, it's gone.

"I'm good," she tries to say, though her tongue is sending sharp pain signals to her brain. She must have bitten it. That happens sometimes when the pain takes root and she loses herself against it. Her teeth feel strange and sharp, the way everything does when you bite your tongue.

Nic nods, slowly and cautiously.

"It's gone," Lora informs him again. "I'm good, really."

"Really?" Nic echoes faintly, and Lora's heart sinks.

"Please don't treat me any different," she says softly.

Lora wants to say more, but the words are difficult. The only times it's harder to speak are when she's sick and when she's Dog.

Dog, Lora's brain skips on the thought, and she—

136

Jaws locked around Dog's throat. Teeth sunk into hers.

It was just a nightmare. It was just a nightmare. Just a nightmare—

"Lora," Nic says like he's talking to a skittish horse, though from the expression on his face, Lora can't tell which of them he's trying to reassure. "Can you look at your hands? Please?"

Obediently, Lora looks down.

"Oh."

The sound comes out as a bark, her vocal cords relaxing under the lighter load of a single syllable.

Her hands—her hands are human paws. Her thumb is twisted backwards and reinserted like a multi-jointed dewclaw. Her hands and wrists are covered in patchy fur, her nails have been replaced with vicious claws, and Lora has no doubt, as she watches the terrible wolf carve up the tree in her mind, that her hands would do any damage she asked of them.

Her teeth—Lora checks again, running her tongue over a veritable mess of canines and incisors—her teeth are *fucked up* in a way that even becoming a dog hasn't done to her before.

A branch breaks in the woods, and Lora feels a new ear, a dog-like ear atop her head, twitch to follow the sound. All of her senses are sharp enough to cut her, and she looks back at Nic, who hasn't stopped his slow, repetitive nodding.

"Oh," Lora says again. "New."

"New," Nic repeats.

{Told you,} the Wolf rumbles in her ear. *{Strong. No laughing. We can do wonders of things.}*

A whine builds in Lora's throat, and she draws her knees up to her chest, rolling onto her side and freeing something that whips and lashes in the space behind her.

Tail, her overloaded human brain offers in a vain attempt at catching up.

Lora looks at Nic. Nic looks at Lora.

"Well," Nic says shakily. "I hope Art didn't hear you, or he's likely to be on his way with a sword."

———–◆◇◆–⁺⚹⁺◆◇◆–———

It takes them several hours of meditative breathing, all of Lora's knowledge on grounding oneself in one's body, and three-to-four hundred empty reassurances, parroted back and forth between them, but by the time they head back to camp, Lora's *situation* has been contained to one wolf ear, one fur-covered human ear, the hastily stitched-together scar on her cheek, and some unusually sharp canine teeth.

They needn't have bothered. Art barely looks up as they re-enter the camp.

"Good!" he announces. "Nothing tried to eat you today."

Nic and Lora exchange glances. Art has turned the camp into a mess of maps, spread in a massive semi-circle around the fire. The contents of his bag are spilled across the grass, and his hands are full with some sort of contraption made of wire, twine, and sticks.

"You've been busy," Nic remarks as Lora makes a beeline for her bedroll.

"Yeah, well," Art answers. "Can't let the sun set on our inaction, right?"

Nic frowns. "I don't think that's the phrase."

"Does it matter?" Art holds up the contraption. "I think I've found an answer."

"An answer?" Nic repeats.

"Yeah, see—"

Art launches into an explanation, and Nic tries his best not to tune it all out as nonsense. Something about the sending stone and resonance and amplification and triangles?

Art doesn't seem to notice his confusion, eventually beckoning Nic over to hold up different parts of the assembly as Nic fights off the swell of homesickness. It looks like something his sister would build, all angles and spellwork and tape.

"Lora, do you want to come see?" Art calls. "I'm about to thin the membrane between our pro and urcosms and send a message across!"

"Mmmmm?" Lora calls back, and Nic steals a worried glance in her direction. "I'm good, thanks."

"Are you sure?" Art insists. "This is groundbreaking speculation!"

Lora sighs and slinks over to join them. She's stuffed her ears and a good amount of hair under a knitted beanie, and settles herself cross-legged on the ground with her chin in her hands to watch.

Art carves several runes in the dirt and works up a paste of spices and other powders, diluting and stretching it like dough around the sending stone.

Nic's eyes amble to the trees. There's something dangerously still about the forest, and he registers suddenly that he's not sure he's seen a single bird, squirrel, or rabbit since they left the real woods behind and stumbled into this shadow copy.

"Here we go!"

Nic's wandering thoughts are cut short by Art's excited cry. A low humming cuts through the air, and Lora winces and covers her ears. Art chants a couple of words that Nic wouldn't dream of trying to spell and places the sending stone in the fire.

It sits there for a moment, unbothered, before catching fire with a flash. The humming stops, replaced with a gust of wind that sends the campfire dancing wildly.

Lora tentatively uncovers her ears, and the three adventurers look at each other.

"Um," Art says. "We're trying to reach Jacob Lantlit? It's the three adventurers he hired. We've discovered the source of the disturbance in—"

There's a sharp *crack* and the sending stone splits down the middle. The three of them startle, staring in horrified, communal silence.

Finally, sadly, Art speaks. "Can't make an omelette without breaking eggs."

Lora whines, and Nic looks over to discover that she's shifted again, becoming nearly fully wolf-shaped this time—though no less of a horror to look at as teeth burst through her cheek and void leaks from her snout like drool.

The Lora-wolf lays on the ground with the end of her nose buried under her paws.

"Dammit," Nic swears, and looks back to Art, who is backing up and staring at Lora's new form in abject terror.

"What," he says, voice shaking, "In the cosmic horror *fuck* is that."

CHAPTER 12

Art isn't thrilled with their explanation of what's going on, especially when Lora gets snappy and defensive, baring her crowd of teeth when he demands to know what happened.

Nic has to agree that on paper *"a werewolf who used to shift into a cute dog but now has several forms, most involving enough muscle and claws to shred a tree into woodchips, all ranging from vaguely unsettling to downright horrifying"* looks pretty bad, but when they finally drag the vaguest of explanations from Lora, he gets it.

"I chose this," she growls. "I'm a godsdamned adult, and I'm the same person you were fine with yesterday, so get your fucking shit in check."

Nic gets it. He hates it, but he gets it.

He likes Art, but there's something in the other boy's eyes that makes him think of expectations, of sweating through long pants in the summer because his choices were heatstroke or a skirt, of taking scissors to his hair and lying to his mother that the resulting length was an accident.

So he goes to bat for the girl he wanted to strangle a couple of days ago, and he tries to remind himself not to write Art off completely in the process.

Breakfast is tense. Lora dances between human and wolf-shapes, each change revealing a new horror. Her wolf-form doesn't seem to care much for talking, content to slink and writhe in the dirt until the gaps between its ribs are full of grass and uprooted weeds.

Art glowers into his plate, scribbles in a notebook, and pretends not to hear Nic's attempts at conversation.

How did it all go wrong?

Nic immediately knows the answer. The woods are toying with them, batting its prey around before it swallows them alive.

Nic doesn't like being prey, but he doesn't have the luxury of a wolf god appearing in his dreams at night with a new body either.

A sound from Lora draws his focus, and Nic turns his head in time to see her sit up, her whole wolf-body rigid with attention. She sniffs the air, ears twitching.

"What is it?" Nic asks, scanning the trees for anything amiss.

Lora stands, stalks a few steps.

"Lora?" Nic says again.

Lora looks at him, pupils dilated into vast black pools. And then she bolts off into the woods.

Nic casts a look at Art, and the other boy mutters a petulant, "Go after her if you want."

So Nic takes off running, drawing his blade as he goes.

He doesn't have a shot at keeping pace with Lora, not while she has four legs and he has two, but the sounds of startled shouting from up ahead, followed immediately by crashing bushes and loud cursing, make her easy enough to follow.

When he catches up, she's sprawled on the chest of a tiefling who has stopped spewing expletives long enough to stare at her, jaw dropped to his chest.

"What the fuck?" he stammers eloquently before spotting Nic. "Hey, what the fuck? Call off your dog!"

In a blink, Lora has shifted into the most human form Nic has seen her manage all day, still straddling her prey in a way that feels far too intimate for the situation.

"Tobias!" She chirps. "Hi!"

The tiefling's jaw drops further, a feat Nic didn't believe possible. "*Lora?!*"

Lora grins, disturbing the mostly-normal, mostly-girl

vibes by revealing, once again, entirely too many teeth. "What're you doing?"

"I—" Tobias stares. "You know, when I said we should catch up if we found ourselves on opposite sides of the bar from each other again, this isn't exactly what I was picturing."

Lora rolls her eyes, shifting wolfwards again.

"What're you *doing* here, Tobias?" she repeats in a growl like tumbling rocks.

"I'm on a job," Tobias admits, letting his head fall back onto the ground with a soft *thump*. "Or rather, I was *assigned* a job, and now I'm stuck in here. What happened to you?"

"Got a job!" Lora beams, tail lashing behind her. "Found it at the post office like you said!"

Tobias nods slowly. "And the rest?"

Lora grins again, tumbling off of him and shifting mid-roll to land on two human legs.

"This is Nic," she announces. "Nic, Tobias."

"Charmed," Tobias deadpans, pulling himself up to a sitting position. "He and him pronouns. Yourself?"

"The same," Nic answers carefully, tucking his blade away. "Woods got you too?"

Tobias spreads his hands, gesturing to the surrounding trees as if to say *obviously*.

"I've just been wandering," he says instead. "Y'all?"

"We've got a camp set up over that way," Nic answers, dodging the real question. "You alone?"

"I work solo," Tobias affirms.

"Then how do you two know each other?" Nic asks.

Lora makes a strange sound in the back of her throat and blushes when both boys turn to look at her.

Tobias smirks. "Just from around."

Nic's eyes narrow, but he doesn't press the issue and extends a hand to help Tobias up.

"We've got one more in our crew," Nic says. "And we should get back."

———-•◇•+⁘+⁘✳+⁘+•◇•-——

"Who's this?" Art asks as Lora and Nic cross the threshold of the camp with Tobias in tow. Lora, quadrupedal and wolfish again, huffs and starts clawing at the dirt.

"Tobias Macaulay," Tobias says smoothly. "He/him. Friend of Lora's."

Art's eyebrows raise. "Which Lora?"

Lora growls.

Tobias's brow furrows, and he tips his head towards

her. "That one?"

Art eyes him silently, sizing him up.

"You got a name?" Tobias asks dryly. "Pronouns? Or just that scowl?"

"I thought Lantlit wasn't sending any more adventurers," Art says. "Or children."

"This is Art," Nic intervenes pointedly. "He's not usually this frigid."

Art rolls his eyes.

Tobias gives a world-weary sigh. "I don't deal with Lantlit, so he didn't send me. As to your second point, I don't know what you're referring to, since I am not a child. Additionally, I've seen things that would turn a man's hair grey with horror, and I'm still here, so I'll thank you not to continue insulting my competence."

Art looks rebuked if not remorseful. "What are you doing here, then?"

"Same as y'all, I'd presume," Tobias responds. "Came in, aiming to travel through. Can't seem to get out."

"More hands might be better," Nic suggests mildly. Art shoots a glare in his direction, but Nic shrugs it off. "We seem to have a common goal at least."

"I'll vouch for him," Lora adds, now sitting cross-legged on the ground.

Art rolls his eyes again, and Nic decides he's had enough.

"Art, can I speak with you?" he asks sharply. "In private?"

Art frowns, but he stands and follows Nic out of earshot of the other two. Tobias watches them with a sharp eye until Nic catches him looking.

"I'm not happy about anything that's happening here," Art says lowly.

"Okay?" Nic responds, foregoing diplomacy in favor of blunt efficiency. "So? Last I checked, we were your team, not your kids. You don't have to be happy about Lora's choices. I'm not thrilled that you broke our sending stone by experimenting on it without asking, but I'm being professional about it."

Art chews on his lip, but he does seem to be considering the point.

"If we're going to get out of here, we're not going to do it by fighting," Nic says, a little more gently. "I know I'm one to talk, but please."

Art sighs.

Nic pushes again. "*Please.* What was it you told me? We all do what we have to?"

Art blinks, confusion apparently getting the better of his bad mood. "When did I say that?"

"At your house, I think." Nic shrugs. "You were talking about finishing jobs. So if what we have to do is work together, politely and cooperatively, in order to finish this job…can you do that?"

Art is silent for a long moment, biting his lip and staring at the trees.

"I'm worried," he says at last. "The variables keep changing. I don't know how to keep everybody safe."

Nic nods. "Okay. I understand that. Do you think you can trust that we're all grown enough to handle our own variables?"

Art stares at the trees some more.

"That'd be nice," he finally concedes.

"Good." Nic nods again. "Seriously, you can be pissed off if that's what you need, I guess. But it seems like it's about something bigger than Lora turning from a lycan dog into a lycan wolf."

"What?" Startled, Art tears his eyes away from the trees to look at Nic.

"The dog?" Nic repeats, equally confused.

"Yeah," Art nods. "Lora's dog."

"No…" Nic says slowly. "The dog *was* Lora."

Art stands there, frozen, and Nic watches the calculations run across his face.

"Oh," he says at last. "I… might have overreacted."

Nic shrugs, making a sympathetic face. "Happens. You going to be okay?"

"Probably." Art sighs and scrubs at his face with his hands. "I'm going to take a walk. See if I can get my head on straight again."

"Okay." Nic nods, patting him on the shoulder. "You do that. Just be careful."

"You too," Art responds. He points over to where Tobias and Lora sit, apparently catching up. "Something feels off. I just can't figure out what it is."

"One move at a time," Nic answers. "Go. We'll still be here when you get back."

— - ◆ ✦ ◆ ✦ ✦ ✦ ◆ ✦ ◆ - —

Art doesn't have a destination in mind when he sets out walking. He doesn't have a distance, either. Just the vague idea that he'll walk until his legs get halfway to tired and then turn back with just enough energy to retrace his steps to camp.

If all goes well, the walk will burn off enough nerves that the roiling irritability under his skin will settle, at least for the night.

So, Art breathes in the air, stuffs his hands in his pockets, and walks.

His mother used to send him out like this when he was younger. With five brothers, all younger, there wasn't a lot of room for him to be a problem at home. Whenever he started getting antsy or anxious, she'd send him into town with instructions to come back when he'd walked it off.

When he crossed cosms the first time, it was an accident. When Art landed in the world of Taunneau, he turned his terror into training. His teammates eventually caught on, and Ilsa became a regular sparring partner.

He misses them. He misses Jordan's jokes, Nadia's cooking, and Ilsa's wit.

Art misses Ilsa's everything.

His recent dreams have been worse than usual and, although Art hates to admit it, they've been affecting him. It's been six years, but the single kiss that he and Ilsa shared before everything went to shit still plays in his head, sending a rush of heat across his chest and shoulders no matter how hard he tries to ignore it.

It doesn't matter. Art kicks at the dirt, sends a rock skipping along the grass, and pauses in his walk to watch it.

It hops across the ground and then abruptly disappears.

Art blinks, pauses, and looks closer.

The portal is nearly invisible to anyone standing more

than a few steps away. The forest air shimmers like a gauzy curtain, humming to life as Art approaches. He reaches out a hand, and suddenly the clearing is lit up with purple energy.

Art's blood runs cold.

Barely an arm's length away, the fabric of reality has torn, and Art can see through to the other side.

Art peers closer. It looks like…

Fields, their edges high with growing corn. Cattle grazing. A river, glistening with the leaping backs of freshwater fish as they migrate along their springtime course.

It looks like home.

Not Addersford, the place of his birth and raising, which stopped being home as soon as he was old enough to see the cracks in it.

Taunneau.

Art's mind is racing as he processes. What had Lora said about her new form? She *wanted this*?

Isocosms can form naturally; Art knows this from his studies. There's nothing inherently moral about their makeup, and rules as basic as gravity can vary from cosm to cosm.

What's to say that this isn't a place with sentience? A sphere which, sensing the inner turmoil and pain of its occupants, is gifting them the chance to fulfil their deepest desires?

Art steps closer, almost without noticing it. A warm breeze gusts over him, the smell of cinnamon and pine nearly bowling him over with longing.

"They'll be fine," Art whispers to himself, trying to believe it.

After all, if Lora took her gift, why shouldn't he?

This is different, the rational part of him responds. *She didn't leave. They need you. You promised Nic.*

Art chokes out a painful laugh. *I promised Nic I'd stop hurting them. What better way than by taking myself and my trouble out of their equation?*

It's different, rationality insists. *Dangerous.*

Art is tired of being rational. He's tired of pretending he doesn't *want* and *miss* so badly that it turns him inside out with longing.

He runs a thumb along the portal's fraying edge, rejoicing in the static buzz against his thumb.

This is real, everything in him agrees. Only one question remains.

What is he going to do about it?

Chapter 13

When Art doesn't come back by lunchtime, Nic and Lora start to worry.

Lora stays mostly-human and sits on the ground with her legs crossed and her arms wrapped across her chest, casting furtive glances into the forest every few minutes.

"I'm sure he's just walking," Tobias offers, trying to be helpful. "Maybe he got lost?"

"Maybe he's dead," Lora whines.

By mid-afternoon, they agree that it's time to send out a search party. As none of them feel particularly keen on going out alone, they go together.

"So," Nic asks Tobias as Lora follows Art's scent along the ground, "What kind of work do you do?"

"Classified," Tobias answers with an apologetic grimace. "Nothing exciting, really. Mostly easy jobs for rich employers. Paperwork and noncompetition clauses and such. Lots of traveling."

"Yeah?" Nic says. "Ever cross paths with a prophetic blade?"

"A few," Tobias hums. "They turn into collector's items once they've done whatever they're here for."

Nic nods. "But none with a pending prophecy attached."

"Nah." Tobias laughs. "I stay far away from that shit."

Nic frowns. First Art's dismissal and now Tobias's disdain. "What's wrong with prophecies?"

"Well, nothing," the tiefling concedes. "*If* you're on the right side of them. And that's a big if, even if you're supposed to wield it. Nine out of ten times, they end with people getting dead, and that's just not my scene."

Nic sighs and drops the subject, turning to their wolfish companion.

"Lora?" he asks. "Find anything?"

Lora whines and shifts back to mostly-human, balancing on her heels.

"He's all over the place," she complains. "And then he disappears here, where it smells like—"

Lora tips her head back and sniffs the air for a moment before letting out a disgruntled huff.

"Like *something*," she finishes. "Something familiar, but it's faint, and I keep losing it. It's all in my nose now, and I can't distinguish his trail from it."

Nic sighs, massaging his forehead where a migraine is beginning to bloom as Lora viciously scrubs at her nose with the back of her hand.

"I'm sure he'll come back," Tobias suggests gently. "Or, as frustrating as it would be to still be stuck here without him, maybe he got out entirely. The forest swallows people. Why couldn't it have spit him back out?"

"Excuse me," Lora rumbles. She shifts wolfwards again, stalks a few feet away, then throws back her head and howls, loud enough that Tobias winces and Nic has to cover his ears.

"You need to go for a run or something?" Tobias offers once the howling has stopped.

Lora shifts back into herself, glaring at both of them. "No."

"If *you* can't even find him," Nic concludes, trying to keep the sharpness from his tone, "We don't stand a chance. I agree with Tobias. If Art's still here, he'll come back to camp eventually."

"And if he's not?" Lora retorts.

"Good for him," Nic snaps. "He better be on his way back with some kind of help."

They walk back to the camp in silence. When they get there, Tobias shares the rations he's been traveling with, and they sit around the fire until the stars come out.

Art doesn't come back.

Eventually, they succumb to the persuasion of sleep. Tobias offers to take first watch, Nic snatches up third, and Lora settles for second.

Lora curls up immediately, but Nic doesn't feel like sleeping and takes a seat on the watch-log next to Tobias.

"What's up?" Tobias asks without looking up, still sketching in his notebook.

"Me, apparently." Nic grumbles.

Tobias laughs. "Not tired?"

"Tired enough, just not in the mood for sleeping."

Tobias nods solemnly. "Nightmares."

Nic gives a reluctant shrug.

"You want to talk about them?"

Nic sighs, and Tobias changes tactics.

"You could tell me why you're so interested in prophecies, maybe?" he tries again.

"I…" Nic hesitates. "I don't really talk about it."

"You don't usually get trapped in extracosmal woods, either," Tobias hums. "Maybe you should try. Might take some of the sting out of those nightmares."

Nic's eyes drift to the dark woods, his mind a thousand miles and at least one cosm away.

"I…" Nic starts again, and the words come slowly, though he feels compelled to speak them. "I had a prophecy. About me. Maybe. Or, we thought it was about me. Everybody thought it was about me."

Tobias closes his sketchbook, setting it aside and focusing his attention on Nic. Nic keeps his focus on the woods, knowing he'll lose his courage if he can see Tobias any clearer than out of the corner of his eye.

"It was a couple generations old. Said the oldest… well, the oldest daughter from my mother's bloodline would someday defeat a great evil come to defy our god and destroy our town."

Nic can feel the other boy's eyes flash over him, but he doesn't speak.

"I'm not a girl," Nic says slowly, surprised at the lump swelling in his throat. "But my mother would never have let me be anything else."

Tobias makes a sympathetic noise. He places a hand on Nic's arm, and Nic does his best not to shake it off, fighting against every instinct in his bones.

"By the time *I* figured it out, it was too late. I was committed. And really, who was to say the prophecy wouldn't be transphobic, or sexist, or any number of things along that vein?"

Nic pauses, clearing his throat. Tobias passes him a flask, and Nic doesn't ask what's in it before taking a long drink. It's water. He would have taken something stronger too.

"I couldn't put all my faith towards hoping the prophecy was wrong," Nic admits at last. "I didn't have enough left. So, I decided that I must be wrong, or that it would be fine if no one knew. Stuffed everything in a box and never told anyone except my sister once in a moment of weakness. I told her to forget it afterwards. She didn't. So, when I…"

Nic swallows, taking another long draft from the flask.

"It was probably about her, the whole time," he finishes. "She saved everyone, including me, and I left town without telling anybody what they had gotten wrong."

Memories flash through Nic's mind, and he's surprised to find himself indulging them.

Cutting his hair in the reflection of a river, two days out from home, and watching the stream carry it back without him. Continuing on, free of its weight.

His sister, hunting Nic down to wrap him up in a hug and a cloak made of scales from the dragon's hide.

"We slew it together," she says, eyes shining with tears.

Showing up at the Tayags' doorstep, the name "Nicodemus" rolling off of his tongue like he hadn't been practicing for miles. Offering to help with their farm in exchange for food in his belly and a roof over his head.

Meeting Beau. Planting turns to harvest, then planting and harvesting again. The Tayag family accepts him without question, until—

Tobias lets out a long exhale, drawing Nic back to the present.

"That's shit luck," he says. "I'd be having nightmares too."

Nic draws in a shaky breath. "Yeah?"

"*Yeah.*" Tobias looks at him like he's grown a second head. "All that shit? It's some heavy-duty trauma, my man."

Nic waves the observation off. "Not more than anyone else. I mean, my mom—"

"Hey," Tobias interrupts. "With respect, I don't give a fuck what your mom went through. You don't treat your kids like that. My dad didn't bat an eye when I came out. That's the way it ought to be."

Nic frowns, eyes drifting to the trees again.

"Go sleep," Tobias says, picking up his sketchbook

again. His pencil dances over the page, and then he tears it out, folding it into precise quarters before handing it to Nic. "I don't know any spells for good dreams, but this should keep away some of the bad. Put it in your pocket or under whatever you're resting your head on."

Nic takes the paper, running his thumb along the edge.

"Thank you," he says at last. "I appreciate it."

Tobias flashes him a half smile, then shoos him away. "Lie down at least if you can't sleep. It's better for you."

"You sound like my partner," Nic scoffs, rolling his eyes. "Y'all take a course in '*Reassuring Failed Heroes of Lore*' or something?"

"Go." Tobias laughs, and Nic obeys.

He slips the sigil in his pocket and, for old time's sake, sends up a prayer to any god who might be listening.

Please. Let me get some fucking sleep tonight.

Nic rests his head on the ground, slides his folded hands under his cheek, and closes his eyes. His body aches for the smell of hay, the soft flannel of heirloom quilts, and the warmth of Beau's embrace.

As he drifts, one more memory flits unbidden across his mind, and Nic, too sleepy to resist, watches it play.

Nic and Beau, announcing their engagement. Silence

fills the kitchen as the Tayags look at each other and then at their son. No one looks at Nic, and he holds his wings steady against his back.

"Really?" Beau's father asks, reluctance in every line of his expression. "The two of you?"

"You could congratulate us," Beau says, his grip tightening on Nic's hand. "You've been hounding me about marriage since I turned seventeen."

"You have to understand," his mother jumps in. "We thought you would settle down with... someone we knew. One of the girls from town?"

Her words cut straight through Nic, through breakfasts and jokes and festivals and apple picking, straight to the part of him that keeps his shirt on during hot days in the fields, declines swimming in the summer, and hides panic attacks in the barn.

He covers the sting with forgiveness. This is hard for them. What else can he do?

"You do know Nic!" Beau protests, and Nic offers a tremulous smile, waiting for the ground to swallow him whole. Maybe under layers of roots and dirt, he will finally belong.

"We're happy for you," Mr. Tayag says, looking like he's swallowed a peach pit. "We're just surprised."

Lora makes a noise in her sleep, and Nic rolls over, wiping the tears from his eyes before they can fall.

CHAPTER 14

Sleep seizes Lora quickly, and when she opens her eyes, she finds herself in the forest once again. This clearing is bathed in moonlight and snow, and before her, seated regally on the ground, is the wolf she rejected.

The white wolf eyes Lora indifferently, and Lora can feel a dozen emotions warring for attention. She closes them behind a door and crosses her arms.

"You're alive," she says softly. "And alone."

The moonlit wolf blinks slowly, like a cat. "So are you."

"I chose the other one. I watched—I felt—" Lora pauses to collect herself. "You shouldn't be here. Why are you here?"

The wolf laughs, bright as a bell. "These are my woods. I am not so small that a rejection of one offering *will kill me. The veil is thin. Why have you come?"*

"I didn't," Lora responds, frowning. "I don't have a say in what I dream about."

"Don't you?" the wolf asks.

Lora's frown deepens into a scowl, and she turns to leave.

"Do you know where you're going?"

The wolf is at her side, though Lora didn't see her cross the distance.

"It doesn't matter where I'm going. This is a dream. You're not real, the woods aren't real, the—" Lora flounders for a second before stabbing a finger in the direction of a normal looking pine. "That tree isn't even real. They're all echoes. I made my choice, and I'm leaving."

"I see." The wolf continues to keep pace with Lora's steps. "How have you enjoyed your choice?"

"It's great," Lora snaps. "I'm useful and strong, like I'm supposed to be. I don't get tired, and I don't feel any pain."

"Mm," the wolf hums. "Sounds lovely."

"It is," Lora retorts. "It's perfect."

A howl rings through the woods, and Lora freezes. The wolf keeps walking.

"Perfect is a heavy word."

"What's that?" Lora asks.

The wolf lifts her nose, sniffing delicately, and Lora subtly does the same. The scent on the wind is familiar, achingly so, of earth and rain and wet fur. And then, on the tail of the breeze... blood. Enough blood to drown out everything else.

"What do you think it is?" The wolf counters, settling down again, tail spread like a pool of moonlight beside her.

"They're your woods," Lora snaps. "What's here?"

"Well," the wolf says softly, fixing Lora in her unblinking gaze as the thing in the distance howls, "You're here. And it seems you've brought a ghost."

Lora's blood runs cold, and she closes her eyes tightly as the sound of howling fills her ears. A new howl joins the mix, and Lora's eyes fly open again.

"Welcome back, sister," the terrible wolf purrs.

The moon is gone, and the white wolf is gone, and the trees are on fire, red flames licking at the tops of charcoal trunks.

"What happened to the trees?" Lora asks as the crackling fire drowns the howling out.

The wolf casts its gaze about and rolls one massive shoulder in a shrug. "They've always been like that."

"They weren't a moment ago."

"Why have you come, sister?" the wolf asks. "To show off? To thank me? I am hungry for excitement, but I did not give you anything you did not have before."

"I don't know," Lora whispers, opting for the truth. "I didn't mean to come."

"Regardless, you are here."

The howling rings out again, and the wolf bares bloody, yellowed fangs. "Shall I take care of that? Or will you?"

"He's just a ghost, right?" Lora says. "He can't cause any harm."

"I do not like my woods to be full of others' ghosts," the wolf growls. "You cannot run forever."

"I know," Lora whispers.

"Then go," the wolf rumbles. "Take your ghosts with you."

Lora ducks her head and turns to leave. Without warning, the terrible wolf appears before her, its nose pressed to hers.

"Lora," the terrible wolf says as gently as a monstrous thing like it can. "That which is gone will only disappear once you release your hold."

Lora flinches, closing her eyes against the threatening tears.

"Goodbye, sister." Warm breath washes over her as the wolf drags its ruined tongue along her jaw. "You will not return."

There is a great tearing of wind, and when Lora opens her eyes, she is in a tree. Bloody paws have left tracks in the snow below her, carving out a trail, and Lora shivers in the chill.

"I'm sorry," she whispers to the air as icy tears crystallize on her cheeks and nose. "I didn't mean to hurt you."

Something shifts at the base of the tree, a bloody mess of teeth and fur, and Lora holds her breath.

Dog sniffs weakly at the air and buries his head in his side, licking at the wound.

Don't, Lora wants to say, but she holds the words behind her teeth.

She did this. She wanted all of this.

Lora buries her face in her arm to smother a cry, pressing both hands over her ears as Dog lets out another mournful howl.

"Stop," Lora sobs, closing her eyes and willing herself to wake up. "Stop, stop, stop."

The clearing fades, and Lora tumbles through the darkness until she wakes.

[Nicodemus.]

Nic opens his eyes. Everything is dark. He stands in a viscous void. A ball of light pulses in the center of the space, golden and orange and pink, and Nic looks down at himself. He can see his body dimly, dark shadows twining around his limbs and chest, but the pulsing light keeps them at bay.

*[**Nicodemus Ananda Miles,**] the voice says again. [**Your second name means Peace. If you seek it, come closer. We have little time.**]*

Nic steps forward.

"Who are you?" he asks, and his voice is drawn into the light and dissolved. "How do you know me?"

*[**I know all. You seek the blade of Imlin.**]*

Nic's breath catches in his throat.

"Who are you?" he asks again, desperate.

*[**You have known my name, if not my face.**] the voice responds. [**Your parents call me Tumelnin. Your sister calls me Tumes when she is swearing. You are known to me.**]*

Nic falls to his knees, and the light pulses stronger, urgency radiating off of it in waves.

*[**We do not have time for worship, nor do I require it. You are at the very edges of my reach. I cannot help you here. It was difficult enough to speak to you like***

this. Do you seek peace, as the name you kept suggests? Do you seek victory, as the name you have chosen implies?]

"Why?" Nic breathes. "What do you require?"

[Answer me, first.]

"Yes. I—I do. Is this real?"

[What proof would convince you?] Tumelnin's light throbs, impatient. **[I am real, as are you. My power is weak here. I cannot perform miracles.]**

"I'm sorry," Nic begs. "You're just... so different. I never thought—"

[My followers are mortal. Thus, the pictures they paint of me are flawed. They know divinity through the lens of death, and death—when feared as they fear it— corrupts.]

Nic bows his head. "I'm sorry. I'm scared."

The light reaches out, and Nic feels warmth on his face.

[For what little it is worth to you,] the god of his childhood hums, **[I am sorrowed by what was done to you in my name.]**

The dam breaks, and Nic weeps. The light envelops him, burning away his tears.

[I will do my best to leave a mark, that you may have assurance of this meeting,] Tumelnin whispers. **[For *now, I will convey my message. Imlin's blade is what you seek, balm to the land you love. A soldier wields it now, and you will know it by my mark on the pommel.]*

The light flashes brightly, and when Nic looks behind him, the shadows are alive, writhing and wreathed in flames and forming the burning shape of a star with two long ends.

[Be well, Nicodemus. Time is short.]

"Wait!" Nic calls, grasping at the air.

He is too late. The light withdraws, and Nic swallows his sobs as he is left in the dark once again.

Chapter 15

When Lora wakes in the morning and there is still no sign of Art, she decides to take charge. Lora is, despite recent best efforts by the cosms to dissuade her, still an optimist, and part of that means committing herself to hope.

"Art got out," she announces, striding up to where the boys have sat down to have breakfast.

Nic and Tobias look at each other, then back at her.

"How do you know?" Nic asks. There's a smell of fire about him, and Lora sniffs, wrinkling her nose.

"It's the only thing that makes sense. I've been thinking more. His smell didn't get drowned out, there was just no more of it. What makes more sense—that he stood somewhere for a minute and stopped creating human smell before heading jauntily off into the inescapable woods with plans to avoid us forever, or that *he escaped the woods?*"

Nic sighs. "It's sounder than most of the logic we've been following."

"So, what's the next step?" Lora goes on. She doesn't give the boys time to respond before answering her own question. *"We* escape the woods."

"I might be able to help with that," Tobias offers. "I'm no expert, but what magic I have is at your disposal."

"Can you make a teleportation spell?" Lora asks.

Tobias grimaces. "I mean… I could try to cobble something of that size together, but I'd need ingredients, as well as something *from* wherever we're trying to get back to. I'm assuming that's Glenhurst, but it can't just be something that's been there. It needs to be an object with memory of the place, something that's itching to get back."

Lora deflates. "I don't suppose a napkin from the tavern will cut it?"

"No." Tobias shakes his head. "Napkins are transient, with short memories. They're meant to be used and disposed of. I could *maybe* send a message on a napkin, but it'd be more likely to burn up in the spell's energy than go anywhere with it."

"Oh my god," Nic blurts.

"What?" Tobias turns to him. "You're already asking a lot, and to ask it of a napkin is—"

"No," Nic gasps, and Lora cocks her head. He's

laughing, she realizes, doubled over with the force of it. Lora isn't sure she's ever seen Nic laugh like this.

"Are you planning to *share*?" Tobias deadpans.

"No—I—" Nic is practically rolling on the ground, wrestling for something in his coat, and Lora's curiosity is starting to turn towards concern.

"This!" Nic announces, holding up a piece of metal. "It's—It's—"

"'It's?'" Lora repeats.

"Give it here," Tobias demands.

"It's Art's doorbell!" Nic cackles.

Lora blinks. "*What*?"

"Oh, *Tumelnin*," Nic pants with residual laughter, holding his side. "I'm staying with him. I arrived the day before we took this job. It was pouring, and I was impatient, and I pulled too hard and broke part of it off."

"Oh…" Tobias holds the broken doorbell reverently, his fingers gliding over its ridges and whorls. "This is perfect. It's old, tied to a specific location, freshly taken from its other half, *and* it's got some spellwork attached already, so it should withstand a bit more to get it home."

Lora can't stop the grin from spreading across her face, and for once, she isn't sure she cares. "We're going home?"

"I need ingredients too," Tobias reminds them both.

"I'll get what you need," Nic volunteers, getting to his feet.

"Perfect. Lora, you're with me." Tobias sets the doorbell down at last, grabbing his sketchbook and scribbling down a list, a few hasty illustrations sketched beside the item names. "Nic, here. Get double quantities of anything delicate, if you can."

"On it."

Nic jumps to his feet, takes the list, and disappears into the woods. Tobias turns to Lora.

"Can you dig a shallow trench around the campfire?" he asks. "Deep enough to lay your hand flat all the way around, with five handful-sized holes around it?"

Lora nods, setting to work. One shifted wolf paw later, the task is done, and Lora sits herself down on the ground to watch Tobias work.

— — ◆ ◆ ✦ ✧ ✶ ✧ ✦ ◆ ◆ — —

Nic acquires the first set of ingredients with little trouble. The contents of his pockets sound like one of his sister's spellwork assignments:

    1. snail shell, empty

    2. bark, enough to start a fire

    3. moss, any kind is fine as long as it still has dew in it

It's a motley assortment, but Nic's collected stranger. He's reaching for one *"sedimentary rock, fist-sized"* when the air crackles to life with a purple glow.

Nic stares into the portal, and the void stares back.

"Tumelnin?" he ventures.

The portal pulses, and then something reaches out and grabs hold of Nic's arm.

— ‑ ◆ ✦ ◆ ⊢ † ✳ † ⊣ ◆ ✦ ◆ ‑ —

Tobias takes a pen, a jar of ink, and several small pouches from his traveling bag. He picks up the pen first, mumbles a few words, and runs his finger along the length of it. A glimmer of light trails behind his touch.

"What's that?" Lora asks, scooting closer.

Tobias startles, and Lora wonders if he'd forgotten she was still there.

He must've expected the digging to take longer, she decides, with no small measure of pride.

"It's a, uh…" Tobias holds the pen up and extends it towards her. "Just a pen, but I've put an enchantment on it to check my work."

Lora takes the pen, examining it visually before giving it a good sniff. It smells like Tobias, like anise and ink and…

Lora's mouth goes dry. *Magic.*

That's what she smelled at the spot where Art's trail went cold in the woods. Not just any magic.

Tobias's magic.

Lora is still processing the revelation when she feels a hand settle on her knee.

"To be truthful," Tobias says softly, "I could've split the list between the two of you."

Lora is still reeling, still fitting together the pieces of a puzzle she didn't know was waiting to be assembled.

"But I wanted some time alone," Tobias goes on. "I didn't expect to see you again, but I'm glad to, despite the less-than-ideal circumstances."

Lora's heart is pounding like a rabbit's, and she looks up, shying away from Tobias's eyes. *What does he know? What could he have done? What is there to hide from us?*

Tobias's eyes search her face for a moment, and then he lets out a soft, understanding, "oh."

"Oh?" Lora repeats, her voice shaking. "What's *oh*?"

"You figured it out." Tobias sighs, taking his hand away and sliding it into his pocket. "I thought you might. I'm sorry to do this."

The words crash against Lora's ears like waves. She dives to one side, instincts screaming to get away from Tobias, to get past him, but she's too slow. There's a burst of glitter and color and light in her eyes and then the smell of something cloyingly sweet.

Fuck, Lora thinks. And then the world goes dark.

CHAPTER 16

Lora surfaces in a dark place. There is no forest, no wolf, no dog, and no moon.

There's a man seated in a red leather chair. Lora cannot focus on his face; it hurts to try.

"Hello," the stranger says. "Who are you?"

"Who are you?" Lora returns. "What are you doing in my dream?"

The man laughs, and a fire springs to life in the empty space behind him. "You may call me Alden. I'd like to be a friend."

Something nags at the edge of Lora's mind.

"I... have to be somewhere," she says, slowly.

"Well," the man hums, "For now, you're here. Might as well sit."

Another chair appears, and Lora steps forward, settling tentatively on the very edge of it.

"You're not a wolf," she observes.

The man laughs again, lightly. "Do you dream of wolves often?"

Lora hesitates.

"Speak freely," the man encourages, and the words tumble from Lora's lips.

"Not often, but lately. I'm lycan, but these wolves are even strange to me."

She tells him everything. When she finishes, the man hums again, tapping one finger against his knee.

"Lora, right?" he asks.

Lora nods.

"I want to help you, Lora."

Lora laughs, the sound weak. "Everyone does, it would seem."

The man chuckles. "What if I could give you a fresh start? What if, when you left this room and these woods, you were free of the weight that everyone has burdened you with. Would you like that?"

He's opened a book, begun to write, and the firelight catches the end of his pen, glittering like a star. Lora's attention is captured by it, the world narrowing to a single point of focus.

"Lora?" the man asks again. "Would you like that?"

"What?"

"Would you like my help?"

"Yes," Lora whispers. "I don't know what I'm doing. I'll take all the help I can get."

"Excellent." The man snaps the book shut, and the sound startles Lora back to the moment at hand. "I'm needed elsewhere, but it was a pleasure, my friend."

"But what—" Lora begins, but the chair across from her is empty when she looks at it.

She is alone in this void with two chairs, a roaring fire, and the sinking sensation in her stomach that she has missed something important.

CHAPTER 17

Nic barely has time to process the hand on his arm before Art tumbles through the portal, knocking Nic to the ground. The veil closes behind him with a loud *pop* of discharged energy.

"Art!" Nic gasps as the wind is driven from his lungs.

Art looks significantly worse for wear. Twigs and leaves stick out of his hair at all angles, and there is a hunted look in his eyes. "Nic?"

"Did you bring help?" Nic asks. "You got out, didn't you?"

Art shakes his head. "Only deeper. It's like a maze, and this is just the entry level."

Nic shudders. "How did you get back?"

"I don't know. I was running through the woods, and then the tear opened. I could see you on the other side, so I dove through before it could change its mind."

Art pulls himself up, extending a hand to help Nic up.

"It was probably coming for me," Nic processes, taking the proffered hand. "They must only show up when we're alone."

"I'm not mad that I was lucky enough to be near it." Art shrugs, and his eyes dart around the woods. "Why are you alone? Where are Lora and the new guy?"

"Oh!" Nic digs in his pocket for the list. "I'm getting spell components. Tobias thinks he has enough magic for a teleportation spell to get us all out."

"Really?" Art frowns. "If he has enough magic and that kind of heavy anchor, why would he ever think he was stuck here in the first place?"

Nic coughs. "The, uh, the anchor's mine, actually. Or, sort of yours?"

Art cocks his head, but Nic brushes off his confusion, passing him the list.

"I've got the first few. With two of us, it should go faster."

"Okay, so—" Art pauses, staring at the list. "What did you say you were getting?"

"Spell components?" Nic repeats. "Ingredients for the teleportation spell?"

Art looks up at him. "You don't know the first thing about magic, do you?"

Nic bristles. "I know some. My sister—"

"Okay, sure," Art concedes. "But… this list is bullshit."

Nic tries to take the paper back, but Art pulls it out of his reach. "No, see? The ingredients are way too broad, while somehow also being too specific?"

"And this one," Art adds, pointing to an item midway down the sheet. "Any spellcaster worth their salt would be carrying this already. This one—I've never seen that grow anywhere that isn't covered in permafrost."

"So… what?" Nic asks, frowning. "What are you saying?"

"I'm saying that either he's lying about his spell— though I can't picture any spell that would require *all* of these components—lying about how much magic he knows, or…"

Art trails off, but Nic has already caught his drift.

"He wanted me out of the way," he finishes. "He might've even wanted me lost or taken deeper into the maze."

Art nods solemnly. "Which means Lora's in trouble."

— - ◆ ✦ ◆ ✦ † ✳ † ✦ ◆ ✦ ◆ - —

Tobias is sweating under his jacket, but the end of the job is so close that he doesn't dare take it off. His bag is packed and slung over his shoulder, his spellwork is written, double-checked, and stuffed in his back pocket. Everything that isn't on his person right now is disposable in the long run.

Lora is still unconscious, which means the clock is ticking. She's been out for about five minutes, and the powder he used should keep her under for another fifteen.

Tobias didn't bother tying her up. It would eat up too much time, and with the wolf form at play, rope isn't even guaranteed to hold her.

Her companion will be wandering the woods until I'm long gone, he repeats, catching himself throwing another anxious glance over his shoulder.

Adrenaline runs through Tobias's veins, and he tosses a handful of blended components into the fire. He doesn't pause to watch the flames roar to life, dancing wildly as the magic feeds them. Instead, he tucks his own anchor into one of the holes Lora has so helpfully dug and sprinkles the rest of the components along the length of the shallow trench.

Ten minutes gone.

He crosses the clearing with quick, precise steps and kneels over Lora's sleeping form. If Patience, his best friend, was here, she would tease him mercilessly for worrying about the consent issues around cutting off a thumb's length of Lora's hair without asking, despite having broken her trust by knocking her out in the first place.

Tobias does it anyway, knotting the curl in the middle and slipping it into a hidden pocket of his bag.

He slices a few strands of his own hair, pulls out his notebook, and slips them in the cover to hold until he's ready. Sliding his favorite enchanted pen from his sleeve, he begins scribbling the words that will take him home.

Eight minutes left.

He's blowing on the ink, about to sign his mark at the bottom, when something bowls him over from the side. His book and pen go flying, and Tobias curses his luck.

———–·◆·—·´·⎯†✳†·´·—·◆·–———

Once Nic and Art enter the clearing, everything starts moving faster.

Tobias kneels over a very still Lora, writing something in his book, and Art lunges at him, tackling the other boy and sending them both tumbling through the grass. Nic breaks into a run, skidding to a stop at Lora's side and frantically searching for a pulse.

He tries to tune out the grunting and cursing sounds of struggle.

Under his fingertips, Lora's pulse beats. *Alive.*

"Hey," he yells. "Art, she's alive!"

"Great!" Art calls back. "I'm a bit busy!"

Nic twists around to check the status of the fight. He's just in time to watch Art slam his fist into Tobias's jaw, sending the other boy to the ground. Art grabs Tobias's arms, pinning them behind his back, and makes eye contact with Nic.

"Rope," Art orders, panting slightly from exertion as he drags a stunned Tobias towards the closest tree. "It should be in my bag."

Nic scrambles for it and helps Art tie Tobias to the tree. The tiefling is out of breath, and he lets out a grunt as his head rolls, making sharp contact with the birch's trunk.

"Who sent you?" Art demands. "What's your role in this?"

Tobias laughs weakly, spitting a mouthful of blood onto the ground.

"Fuck you," he scoffs. "What would I tell you for, huh?"

"Tell me," Art growls. "Or I'll hit you again."

Tobias grins wearily up at him. "Promise?"

Nic grabs Art's arm as the other boy goes to make good on his word.

"You're not going to get anywhere," he hisses in Art's ear. "He's prepared for that. You've gotta find something that matters to him."

Tobias laughs again, pulling against his restraints.

"You tie good knots," he calls to Nic. "Most folks in over their heads are sloppy. I gotta give you credit. Lora's *fine*, by the way. I'm not being paid enough to add murder to my day."

"Ignore him," Nic insists, and Art pulls his arm away with another growl of protest.

Lora starts to stir, and Art stalks to her side.

"Hey," Nic hears him murmur. "You okay?"

"Art?" Lora mumbles groggily. "You came back?"

Art's concern softens. "Yeah, stupid. I shouldn't have left."

Tobias has fallen silent, watching as Nic searches the campground. It's only when Nic's eyes land on Tobias's notebook that he hears the other boy draw in a sharp breath.

Nic scoops the sketchbook up, turning around to see the first shreds of concern in Tobias's eyes.

"Hey, no, hey—" The other boy starts.

"Yeah?" Nic shoots back. "What, is this important to you?"

"No, please," Tobias says, gritting his teeth and

wrestling against the ropes. "Let's not be hasty here, okay?"

"Answer me, then," Nic orders. "What are you really here to do?"

"I can't," Tobias says. "It's not that simple. I—"

Nic tears a page out, and Tobias lets out a pained noise.

"Tell me why you're here."

"Please," Tobias begs. "Please. Don't destroy it. I can fix the pages, but everything I've made is in that book, and I can't—I'm nothing without it—"

"Yeah?" Nic walks to the fire, dangling the notebook over the flames. His words come out tasting like poison and ash. "I think you could stand to be knocked down a peg."

"Please!" Tobias strains against the ropes, his eyes on the flames already licking hungrily at the cover of his book. "We can figure something out. I can help you!"

"*Fuck you,*" Nic says, and lets go.

Lora screams. Art yells. The book falls, and Tobias's face splits into a bloody grin.

"Dammit, Nic!" Art shouts. "The fire is the energy source! Introductory magic says—"

"Don't burn what you don't understand," Tobias

finishes, wheezing with laughter. "Oh, you should see your face."

Art scrambles for the fire, but Tobias only laughs harder.

"Don't bother," he goes on as the pages of the book blacken and burn. "It's in motion now. We'll all get to see what happens next."

"Maybe it'll be fine?" Lora calls.

The ground begins to rumble beneath their feet, shaking and boiling and blistering open. Nic stands frozen by the fire, staring at the mess he's made.

"Hope so, for y'all's sakes," Tobias chirps. "See you around, yeah?"

The tiefling disappears in a flash of smoke, and Nic bolts for the spot where the ropes dangle loosely from the tree.

"Nic!" Art stops him. "Get the bags!"

Nic changes course, gathering up as much of their shit as he can fit in his arms, and Art grabs the rest. He throws it to Lora and grabs Nic by the arm, dragging his shell-shocked companion along. They form a ball, the three of them, hunched on the grass like a living shield over their belongings.

"I'm sorry," Nic whispers as the wind tears at their clothes and hair, blanketing them in soot and ash and leaves. "I'm sorry, I'm sorry, I'm sorry!"

"It's okay," Lora whimpers, clinging to him. "You didn't know."

There's no time to say anything more. Reality crumples around them like paper, and with a scream like a dying star, everything goes dark.

CHAPTER 18

Lora wakes first, dazed on the blackened ground. For a moment, she thinks she's back in the burning woods with snow floating from the sky.

Her nose is quick to tell her otherwise. *Ash.*

Lora drags herself up, drawing in a sharp breath at the sight. The entire taiga has been razed to the ground, turned into a flat plain full of pockmarked craters, downed trees, and broken wagons. Through the ash-laden air, Lora can see other shapes picking themselves up and looking around in bewilderment.

The missing people, she thinks. She hopes.

Art and Nic are waking behind her, and Lora wordlessly pulls them to their feet. Their bags and belongings all seem to have come through with minimal damage.

There is no sign of Tobias.

"Home," Art says wearily.

Nic scoops something off of the ground nearby.

"I broke your doorbell," he says flatly. "I'm sorry."

Art pulls him into a hug.

With nothing else to do, the three adventurers start walking towards town. They've barely reached the edge of the devastation before they are met by a party on horseback. Jacob Lantlit rides the lead horse, followed by six members of the town guard.

Lantlit stares at them, then at the destruction in their wake. His expression is one of shock and poorly disguised horror.

"What did you do?" their employer asks hoarsely.

Art digs in his pocket and chucks the two halves of the broken sending stone at Lantlit, who fumbles to catch them.

"No one's getting lost in that mess anytime soon," Art rasps.

Another look at their faces convinces Lantlit not to press the issue.

At his order, the soldiers dismount, spreading out on foot. Three of them hand off their horses to the weary party, and Lantlit manages something about "thanks for their service" and "payment delivered to Art's residence."

Lora, Nic, and Art don't speak as they ride back to town. They leave the horses with the first guardsman they encounter, and Art leads them to his house.

He opens the door for Nic and Lora, who collapse onto the couch and floor respectively. Through the window, they catch a glimpse of Art lovingly reattaching the doorbell to its other half with the air of someone who has done this many times before.

Art rests his palm against the bell for a moment, whispering something the others can't make out through the glass, then joins them in the living room.

They drag the pillows from the couch and sleep through most of the afternoon.

At dusk, the heroes are awoken by a messenger who stares at Art in awe as the boy signs to accept the promised payment.

Once the messenger has left, Art starts to split the money into thirds.

"I don't need all that," Lora interrupts softly. "Give me a hundred, no silver, and split the rest between the two of you. I'm going home, I think, so I won't have bills or rent."

"Let me cook you a proper meal before you go," Art insists as he passes her the pouch of coins. "It's the least I can do."

Lora accepts both the offer and the coins, and then she

turns to Nic. "What's next for you?"

Nic stares out the window as the streetlamps begin to light. "I have a lead. Tumelnin, my… *god*, I guess, came to me in a dream. I have to find the blade I came for. I can't go home without it."

"Are you sure it wasn't just a dream?" Lora asks.

Nic pulls a piece of paper, folded in quarters, from his pocket and opens it for them. A sigil in smudged pencil has been sketched in the middle, and intersecting with it is the burned mark of an exploding star. He rolls up his sleeve and shows them a similar burn on his wrist. "These were both there when I woke up."

"Well," Art sighs. "You can stay with me for as long as you need."

"Are you sure?" Nic asks. "I destroyed an entire forest. We could've gotten killed."

"We didn't get killed," Lora reminds him gently. "We got out. That makes us square in my book."

"How are you going to tell your family about the wolf?" Art asks.

Lora hesitates and closes her eyes, her forehead wrinkling with concentration. Nothing happens.

"I don't think it's there anymore," she says at last, opening her eyes again. "I can't feel it. I can't reach it."

"Was it real?" Nic asks.

Art glances towards the corner of the room at something none of them can see.

"It was all real," he says. "But the rules are different here. Maybe the wolf couldn't leave with you. Maybe it was a creation of the isocosm, and everything from that world was destroyed in the blast."

"And Tobias?" Nic presses.

"I met him here," Lora says. "In Glenhurst, before. He was real."

"Good." Art nods. "I've got two fists with his name on them if he ever shows his face again."

Art hauls himself up with effort and heads into the kitchen to cook.

"*Gods,* I've missed you," they hear him whisper, as the icebox cracks open.

Faint strains of music drift out into the living room, and Lora slumps back against the deconstructed couch, letting out a deep sigh.

Nic mirrors her, closing his eyes.

In an hour, they'll eat. Tonight, they'll sleep. Tomorrow, they'll send Lora off and start tracking down leads. What happens after that is anyone's guess.

For now, Nic basks in the fatigue of a completed job and drifts off to sleep to the sound of Lora's snores.

EPILOGUE

The world goes dark, save for a single point of light. Tobias makes his way towards it, towards the roaring fire that he knows is waiting.

His employer sits in a red leather chair, watching Tobias's approach with silent eyes.

Tobias stops in front of him, and Alden waves to the empty chair.

Tobias sits. He waits.

His father gives a heavy sigh. "You know what I'm going to say."

Tobias nods. He waits.

"The loss of the taiga is… significant," Alden informs him. "I believe I can placate our associates with the knowledge we have gained, but it won't be easy. Additionally, this is the third notebook I've had to replace for you this month."

"I know," Tobias answers. *"I can find a cheaper distributor—"*

Alden laughs softly. "The notebook is not the problem. Carelessness will kill you, Tobias. Watch yourself. Understand?"

Tobias lets out a breath. "Yes, sir."

"Good," Alden says. "Now, while I go clean up your mess, I want you to practice."

Tobias nods again. "Of course."

"Good work," his father sighs before the dream begins to fade.

Tobias opens his eyes. He is back in his bed, back in his room, back home. A new notebook, bound in blue leather, rests on his nightstand, and Tobias exhales softly, massaging his stiff jaw and feeling the tender bruising protest beneath his thumb.

His father's last words ring in his ears. *"What could you have done better?"*

Tobias rolls out of bed and tucks the new spellbook under his arm. He crosses the room, grabs three heavy tomes from his bookshelf, and spreads everything out on his desk.

He fills three pages with notes and then washes them clean, grits his teeth, and starts again.

Somewhere deep below the earth, a wolf howls.

ACKNOWLEDGMENTS

I have so many incredible people to thank for the way that *The Awakening of Lora Abernathy* came together.

First of all, to one of my favorite authors: Tamara Jerée. Thank you for letting me infodump in your dms about reluctant werewolf girls and complicated gender feelings while I read *A Wolf Steps in Blood*! Yasmine made me realize just how much I missed being Lora, and ignited the desire to write her story down.

Secondly, Nathaniel and Effie at Dragon Bone Publishing. Thank you for taking a chance on my wild pitch and wilder timeline!! TALA would not exist without all the incredible love and support that y'all have showered me with. Here's to the next 3!

Thirdly, Rowan. I created Lora & Dog for your campaign, and although they've taken on different adventures since then, I owe it all to you for giving us somewhere soft and safe to start.

Likewise: Bobby, Sage, Cas, Jojo, Tricia, Ro, Jared, Zoe, Ziel, Eli, and Syd. Thank you for letting Lora, Nic, Art, and Tobias adventure alongside Reykjavik, Andraste, Kalen, Barbie, Caldore, Kiddson, Ian, Ordan, Osword, Varan, Monica, Davi, Murmur, Reya,

Cybele Hemlock (like the plant), Kugaraw, the five skeletal rats, and Naerys.

Sage, I owe you a billion more thanks for all you've done to shape Art and Tobias, but for now: thank you for your excitement, your enthusiasm, your memes, your theorizing & brainstorming assistance, and your friendship, which I treasure above all else.

To my beta readers: Jess, Kate, Sage, Sidney, Rae, Emily, Nate, and Eli, as well as Kienn, Beatrice, Wyrd, Daybe, Theta, Remy, Stasia, Dee, and everyone else on the TALA street team: your excited screaming & unbridled enthusiasm have meant so much to me during this process. The next book is coming soon, I promise!! <3

To Pippi, Alroy, and Bart: Thank you for all the times I sat down to write and you decided it was the perfect time to stick your asses in my face.

To my wife, partner, lover, breadwinner, & best friend, Ziel: Thank you for everything. You laid the groundwork for 90% of the story I was able to tell here, proposed (much better) titles for nearly every book in the series, and CREATED THE WOLVES!! You are my favorite hype person, a brilliant DM, a joy to play alongside (in DnD and everything else), and the unwavering love of my life.

To my therapist, who has steadily, patiently, and gently walked me through every piece of shit I've projected onto these character. Your humor and compassion are a balm. Here's to finishing the whale and (*please dear god*) not finding a dolphin behind it.

Additional gratitude to Beth for talking through my many etymology questions to form cosm theory & the language of speculatism.

Lastly, since these are my acknowledgments, I want to shout out the dm who told me his table was a safe space for queer folks but that I couldn't play Nic because "transgender people aren't really a thing in the setting" and "the bigotry [Nic] might receive" was "not something [he] would be comfortable roleplaying."

I would like to acknowledge that as bullshit. Fuck you to that guy.

To all my marginalized kin: may your bellies be full, your fur warm, and your hearts refreshed as we go out and build a better world.

ABOUT THE AUTHOR

MJ Anthony (they/them) is a queer, trans, and disabled poet + storyteller. Some days they are incapacitated by one (or more) of their disabling conditions. Other days they get to be a caretaker at a local community library, and co-run the poetry imprint Dragon Heart Press with their friend Nathaniel Luscombe. All those days find them living in Boston with their wife, three cats, and a very lovely leopard gecko named Tumbleweed. Micah has a passion for independent publishing, speculative fiction, high pulp orange juice, and unsweetened black tea.

Find them on instagram @themjanthony, or check out their current happenings at mjanthony.carrd.co

Tending Clay; Unearthing Stars
by MJ Anthony

"Today I am learning // to take anxiety by the hand // and teach this trembling, fragile beast // that we are (and yet will be) // okay."

In their debut collection, MJ Anthony navigates a complicated web of intersecting topics such as complex trauma, neurodiversity, lasting illness, and practicing self-love in a body long-alienated from you. Alongside the reader, the author combs tangles into threads and weaves them into a gentler future, reunifying selves and stories both old and new.

Part hurting, part healing, and wholly original, *Tending Clay; Unearthing Stars* is a love letter to everyone living with a broken body or a troubled mind.

ThistleHeart Home
by R.C. Lloyd

*"…And how will you make it out alive
Of this dark body / of these dark woods…"*

ThistleHeart Home is an atmospheric poetry collection that takes your hand and tugs you on a journey through the woods. Come encounter fears and lies, but know you'll be armed with love and light to beat back the darkness.

Son of the Prophet
by Effie Joe Stock

*Torn between his ancestry,
Desperate to change the world,
The son of the prophet embraces destiny.*

Raised in a loving but sheltered Duvarharian home, Thaddeus's tranquil world is upheaved by a dark cloaked figure-one who wants him and his brother dead.

Haunted by impending danger and empowered by whispers saying he may be the Savior of the Dragon Prophecy, Thaddeus and his dragon seek to destroy the cult controlling the academy and Duvarharia's government. But when Thaddeus's trust in a forgotten deity fails to stop the torment of those he loves, he's left with no choice but to pursue a darker power to succeed.

Will Thaddeus free Duvarharia from the evil entrapping the Dragon Riders? Or will his actions shape him into the traitor Duvarharia fears most?

Moon Soul
by *Nathaniel Luscombe*

*"I don't think I can justify it any longer.
I'm going to quit my job."*

August has never been good with change and isn't sure who she is beyond her job of reading memories in the sand. When she comes to the conclusion that she has to quit her job, she's left with an overwhelming sense of emptiness. What follows is the quiet chaos of a girl regaining control over her life on a small desert moon.

Deciding to take a job in the hanging gardens of the Spire, August discovers more to life as she meets new friends, forms a different connection with her home, and faces an unexpected visitor from her past.